R0085545192

01/2018

D0203939

PALM BEACH COUNTY
LIBRARY SYSTEM
3650 Summit Boulevard
West Palm Beach, FL 33406-4198

The Haunting on Heliotrope Lane

Read all the mysteries in the
NANCY DREW DIARIES

#1 Curse of the *Arctic Star*

#2 Strangers on a Train

#3 Mystery of the Midnight Rider

#4 Once Upon a Thriller

#5 Sabotage at Willow Woods

#6 Secret at Mystic Lake

#7 The Phantom of Nantucket

#8 The Magician's Secret

#9 The Clue at Black Creek Farm

#10 A Script for Danger

#11 The Red Slippers

#12 The Sign in the Smoke

#13 The Ghost of Grey Fox Inn

#14 Riverboat Roulette

#15 The Professor and the Puzzle

And coming soon . . .

#17 Famous Mistakes

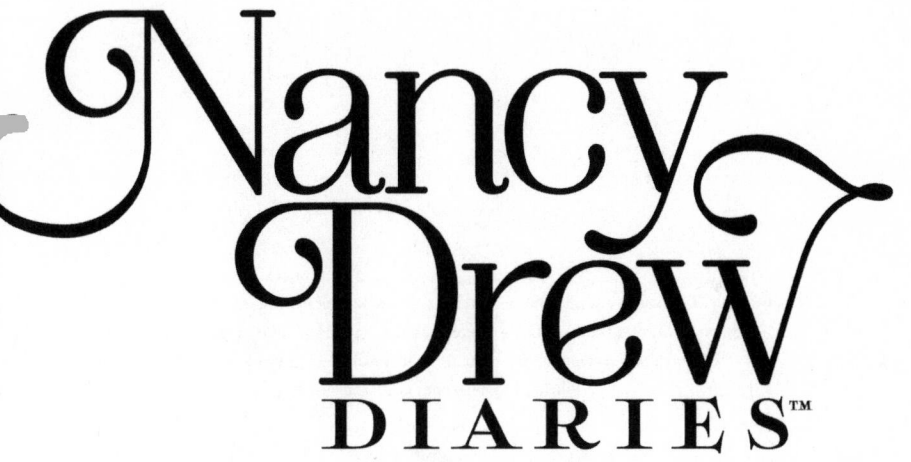

NANCY DREW DIARIES™

The Haunting on Heliotrope Lane

#16

CAROLYN KEENE

Aladdin

NEW YORK LONDON TORONTO SYDNEY NEW DELHI

ALADDIN

An imprint of Simon & Schuster Children's Publishing Division

1230 Avenue of the Americas, New York, New York 10020

First Aladdin hardcover edition January 2018

Text copyright © 2018 by Simon & Schuster, Inc.

Jacket illustration copyright © 2018 by Erin McGuire

Also available in an Aladdin paperback edition.

For information about special discounts for bulk purchases, please contact Simon & Schuster Special Sales at 1-866-506-1949 or business@simonandschuster.com.

The Simon & Schuster Speakers Bureau can bring authors to your live event. For more information or to book an event contact the Simon & Schuster Speakers Bureau at 1-866-248-3049 or visit our website at www.simonspeakers.com.

Series designed by Karin Paprocki

Jacket designed by Nina Simoneaux

Interior designed by Mike Rosamilia

The text of this book was set in Adobe Caslon Pro.

Manufactured in the United States of America 1217 FFG

2 4 6 8 10 9 7 5 3 1

Library of Congress Control Number 2017940051

ISBN 978-1-4814-8547-0 (hc)

ISBN 978-1-4814-8546-3 (pbk)

ISBN 978-1-4814-8548-7 (eBook)

Contents

CHAPTER ONE	The Midnight Show	1
CHAPTER TWO	Haunted	6
CHAPTER THREE	The Sound of Evil	23
CHAPTER FOUR	Haunted House	37
CHAPTER FIVE	Intruders	60
CHAPTER SIX	Who Knows You Best?	74
CHAPTER SEVEN	Another Victim	89
CHAPTER EIGHT	Confrontation	99
CHAPTER NINE	An Invitation	111
CHAPTER TEN	Answers	123
CHAPTER ELEVEN	Guess Who?	131
CHAPTER TWELVE	Showdown	139
CHAPTER THIRTEEN	Scary Movie 2	154

Dear Diary,

I DON'T BELIEVE IN GHOSTS.

Really.

I DON'T.

But every once in a while a case comes along that makes me wonder. Like when Willa told me that her best friend was acting super strange after they went to a so-called "haunted" house on Heliotrope Lane. Once bubbly and fun, suddenly Izzy was acting paranoid, angry—even violent. Willa was afraid her friend might actually hurt her, unless something was done.

Worse, when I went with Bess and George to check out the house, we found it totally trashed by trespassers and lookie-loos. It seemed the rumor that the house was haunted had traveled all through River Heights High School and the middle school. And while the house was totally creepy, I know better than to believe it's haunted.

It just feels like something evil is at work there.

The Haunting on
Heliotrope Lane

CHAPTER ONE

The Midnight Show

"SO, WHEN THE GUY DIED," MY BEST FRIEND Bess Marvin was saying as she walked out of the movie theater, "was that, like, black blood that came out of him? You know, when he was like . . ." She made a retching motion onto the sidewalk.

"Um," I murmured, but my voice was hoarse from three hours of screaming. Freaky Friday double features can do that to you. "Can we talk about something else? *Anything* else?"

But George Fayne, Bess's cousin and my other best friend, had already held up her pointer finger.

"Good question!" she said in her perfectly fine voice. "I thought the black stuff was evil. Like, liquid evil?"

"I thought it was the souls of all the people whose lives he'd ruined," my boyfriend, Ned Nickerson, put in, adjusting his glasses as I thought back to the scene and felt my stomach roil. "You know, by making them eat their own organs. That was *cold.*"

"Oh gosh," I muttered, grabbing my stomach. *I almost forgot that part.*

"Nance!" Bess cried, her blond hair puffing around her shoulders as she stopped short, suddenly taking notice of the state I was in. "Are you okay? You look like you've just seen a ghost!"

"I've just seen *several* ghosts," I reminded her, leaning against a streetlight, "and some zombies, and that one guy with the liquid evil who kind of defies categorization. And a *lot* of carnage." I paused, trying to think about golden retriever puppies, or soap bubbles, or sunshine— anything to counter the three hours of terror I'd just sat through. "Have I mentioned I'm not a horror movie fan?"

"Oh, Nancy," George said, and smiled at me as Ned

put his arm around my shoulders. "I thought you said you were willing to give horror movies a try. I thought *Bess* was going to be the delicate one."

"It's funny," Bess agreed, nodding, "so did I."

"I did give them a try," I said, my voice steadying, "and I think I've decided now. No, thank you. I think I'm done with Freaky Fridays."

"That's kind of unexpected for you, don't you think?" Ned asked. "You're not a scaredy type. You spend half your life chasing bad guys."

This was true. My sleuthing—which had always been my favorite extracurricular activity—*could* get scary, sometimes. "But there's a big difference between confronting a crook and having to eat your own organs," I pointed out.

"True," Bess said, nodding seriously.

"I'm sorry you got freaked," George said, her dark eyes sincere. "I just really wanted to come to this, because you so rarely see Takara movies screened in the United States! And he's such an amazing director. The way he sets up his tension shots . . ."

In the last month or so, George had discovered that she was a huge fan of scary movies. After exhausting her Netflix queue, she'd started checking DVDs out at the library, and then getting recommendations for streaming rentals from horror movie blogs online. She'd become particularly interested in the work of certain directors—like Takara, who, I had to agree, had a real knack for scaring the bejesus out of you. And *maybe* making you a little nauseated.

I took a breath through my nose, breathed out through my mouth. That's how our gym teacher says you should center yourself. "I get it, George. I'm not mad at you. And I can see where the story was cool, if . . . well, if it wasn't going to give me nightmares for the next month. I think maybe I just don't have the constitution for this stuff."

George nodded, smoothing her short black hair behind her ear, and Ned gave me a little squeeze.

"Let's go back to the car," he said. "Turn on all the lights. Play some really fun music, like Lily Jo Jarret."

I smiled. Ned loves Lily Jo Jarret, but he always tries to act like he's listening to her ironically.

"Yeah, we can go back to my house and watch something that's totally the opposite of scary," George suggested. "*Packed House?* I hear that was good!"

Ned took my arm with an encouraging grin and slowly, we made our way around the theater to the parking lot in back. It was huge, nearly empty—and strangely dark.

"Why aren't the lights on?" Bess asked, frowning.

"Yeah," George said, looking around. "The car is over there—I remember where we parked." She led us toward her small red coupe. "But this is weird."

"And probably a safety hazard," Ned added.

"Maybe it's because it's so late?" George suggested, leading us in the direction of the car. She reached into her pocket, pulled out her car keys, and flicked on a little flashlight that was on her key ring. It made a tiny but strong beam of light.

"Maybe," Ned agreed. "They could be trying to save on electri—AAAAAAUUUUUGH!"

A shadowy figure had suddenly jumped into the flashlight beam.

CHAPTER TWO

Haunted

I FELT MY STOMACH LEAP UP INTO MY THROAT and grabbed Ned's arm so hard he cut off his scream to say, "Ow!"

"Oh my God!" Bess screamed, reaching into her purse. *"Get back! I'll get you with my pepper spray!"*

If I hadn't been so frightened, I might have smiled. I've never seen Bess actually use pepper spray, but the threat is always her first line of defense.

"Sorry!" the figure said in a voice that was surprisingly young and female. "Dude, don't spray me. I'm so, so sorry. I didn't mean to startle you guys."

George angled the flashlight at the figure's face. It was a young girl—maybe thirteen or fourteen years old.

She had blond hair pulled back in a high ponytail and wide eyes, and she was wearing a Chicago Bulls hoodie.

"Well, you *did*," Bess said indignantly, pulling her hand out of her purse. "Sorry. I shouldn't have threatened you like that. But maybe don't sneak up on people in dark parking lots after scary movie screenings?"

"I'm sorry, I'm sorry," the girl said again. "You're right, I should know better. It's just, I recognized you, Nancy." She turned to me, hope lighting her eyes. "You're Nancy Drew, aren't you? The sort-of detective? You helped my cousin one time."

"Uh," I said, sort of caught off guard by my unexpected fame. *Sort-of detective? Thank . . . you?* "Probably. I do investigate things sometimes."

The girl looked pleased. "Great. That's great. Oh, I'm Willa, by the way. And again, I'm really sorry I scared you. We just saw the movie, and were walking to the car, and I spotted you and was like, 'Wait, we have to go over—'"

"We?" Ned interrupted, as George moved the flashlight beam to the left and right.

"Yeah," a deep voice intoned from the darkness, making us all jump about a foot in the air.

"How many of you *are* there?" Bess asked the girl, looking nonplussed.

"Just me and my brother," the girl said, and a slightly older boy with a mop of sandy hair stepped into the light, looking less than thrilled to be there.

"Um, *hi*," Ned said, giving him a pointed look.

"Hi," he mumbled. "I'm Owen. Her older brother."

"So, um . . . why were you guys looking for me?" I asked, trying to hurry this along. I was feeling a little silly for getting so freaked out, though honestly I was just happy I hadn't peed myself. That was *scary*.

"Well." Willa looked back at me, cringing a bit. "It's going to sound . . . weird."

"Try me," I replied drily. I've seen a lot of weird things in my time solving mysteries.

Willa glanced over at her brother, though she spoke to me. "I have . . . maybe a mystery for you to solve."

I nodded. "Okay. Tell me more."

Willa raised her eyebrows and went on, "Do you guys know about the house on Heliotrope Lane?"

"The house on Heliotrope Lane?" Bess asked, then giggled. "That sounds funny. It's like one of those old mystery stories—do you remember that series with the yellow covers, Geo—"

"No. What's the deal with the house on Heliotrope Lane?" I asked, cutting Bess off with an apologetic look. *I'm ready to get to the point so I can get home to bed.* I tried to tell her all this with my eyes.

"It's haunted," Owen suddenly piped up. He was staring at his smartphone, his shaggy hair covering his eyes. When he noticed us all turn to stare at him, he looked up. "I mean, *allegedly*," he added.

"What does that mean?" I asked, turning back to Willa.

She glanced at Owen hopefully, as if she thought he might help her explain, but he was lost in his phone again. "Well . . . the house was owned by this older lady, Mrs. Furstenberg," she said slowly. "She wasn't . . . nice. I mean, she was kind of mean to the neighborhood kids, always shooing them off her lawn and yelling at them to be quiet at, like, two o'clock in the afternoon. And she had some crazy number of cats."

"There's nothing wrong with cats," said Bess, who loves her ill-tempered cat, Mr. Checkers.

Willa shrugged. "Sure, yeah, no. The cats weren't the problem. I'm sure she was nicer to the cats than she was to people. Anyway, she lived with her son, who was, like, middle-aged. Henry. Nobody really knew anything about him, because he never talked to anyone. You would just see him in there sometimes, in the rocker in the front room."

George caught my eye. *Creepy,* she mouthed.

"One day, a year or so ago, a neighbor heard a scream," Willa went on. "And he went in to investigate. He found Mrs. Furstenberg dead in this little room in the basement. She'd had a heart attack."

"Okay," I said. This all sounded unfortunate so far, sure—but where was the mystery?

"Henry disappeared that same day. The police looked for him for a long time but never found him. That made them think maybe he knew something about her death."

"Why?" I asked. "You said she died of a heart attack."

Willa nodded. "Yes, that's what the doctors said. But the police thought maybe Henry did something to scare her, or they had an argument that brought on the attack. Anyway, when they couldn't find him, there was nothing they could do, so they just called her death an accident. She didn't leave a will, so the house has been empty ever since she died."

A sudden flash of recognition lit in Bess's eyes. "*Oh*," she said. "Maybe I have heard of this house, from my neighbor Carrie."

Hmmm. "You said the house was haunted?" I asked, looking from Bess to Willa.

"A lot of kids think so," Willa said. "And sometimes,

kids will sneak in there at night to give themselves a thrill."

Ned cleared his throat. "That's a *really* bad idea," he said.

"Yeah," I agreed, "for a lot of reasons, including but not limited to it being against the law."

Willa looked down at the ground. "I know. I mean, we know. Kids know. But you know how it is. . . ."

"Kids do dumb things?" Bess filled in. She glanced at me. "If this is the same house, Carrie *swears* she's never been there, she's only heard about it, but I have my doubts."

I looked at Willa, who I was thinking looked a little more ashamed than just having *heard* about the house called for. "Willa, did you go to the house on Heliotrope Lane?" She didn't respond right away, so I turned to Owen. "Did *you?*"

He scowled and nudged his sister. "Tell them, Willa. That's why we're here, right?"

Willa sighed. "Yeah." She looked at me, her eyes huge and round. "I went a couple of weeks ago. My best friend, Izzy, wanted to go. She's not usually into that stuff, but we both like scary movies, and she thought maybe we could take some video, and it would be like a scary documentary-type thing. Like *Ghost Games*. Do you guys know that movie?"

"I've heard of it," I said, not adding that I don't usually go to scary movies, unless dragged there by my friends.

Willa shrugged. "Too bad she forgot to charge her phone. We didn't get any footage. But . . ." She looked across the parking lot, and suddenly something darker passed over her eyes. *Fear.*

"What happened?" Bess prompted.

Willa shook her head, as if to clear it. "We . . . well . . . we entered on the main floor of the house and looked around, and that was all fine. But then Izzy wanted to go to the *basement*." She looked at us again. "That's where Mrs. Furstenberg's body was found, like I told you. In this little room," she added. "It's where she died."

I nodded. "Right. Sounds scary."

"Yeah." Willa took a breath. "I didn't want to go—I told Izzy no. I may like scary movies, but it was starting to feel like we were actually *in* one. Izzy really wanted to go down there though." She took another breath. "So I told her she could go alone. . . ."

"Okay," I said, when she trailed off. "What happened then?"

"She was gone a really long time," Willa said. "Like fifteen, twenty minutes. I was getting scared. I called down the stairs for her, but no one answered. Finally I realized I had to go after her. I couldn't just *leave* her there." She paused. "I was super freaked out, but I went downstairs. It was dark, and all I had was my flashlight. I was calling her name, and she didn't answer, but I thought I heard this sort of *moaning* sound."

"Yikes," George murmured.

"Yeah, it was pretty scary," Willa agreed. "Finally—it was probably only a few minutes later, but it felt like hours—I found her alone in that little room in the basement, the one where they found Mrs. Furstenberg's body."

"Was she unconscious?" I asked. "Is that why she wasn't answering you?"

"No, that's what's so weird!" Willa replied. "Izzy was conscious, but she was acting strange—she wouldn't say anything. She didn't even seem to recognize me! I was yelling at her, because I was so mad she'd left me and wasn't answering, but it didn't seem to register at all. Finally I just put my arm around her shoulders and started to lead her out of the house."

"Is that like her?" Bess asked. "Being kind of quiet, introspective?"

Owen suddenly snorted. "Not at *all*," he said. "Izzy is the kind of girl who never stops talking. She's ruined so many movies and TV shows for me. She thinks every thought that pops into her head has to be shared."

Willa frowned at him, and he shrugged. "Anyway, when she's around, nobody's getting any work done."

I nodded. "So what did you think was happening?" I asked, turning back to Willa.

"I thought she was fooling around," she said, "but she kept acting that way. We got on our bikes and started riding home, and she seemed to know the way and everything, but she still wasn't saying anything. Finally, when we were a block from Izzy's house, she laughed and made some silly joke about how cold it was. But what's so weird is, when we started talking, I realized she had no memory of even *going* to the house."

George let out a whistling sound. "*Weird*," she said.

"Yeah," I agreed. But my sleuthing mind was already working, and it seemed like there could be a lot of different explanations. Maybe Izzy had hit her head in the basement? Maybe she was angry at Willa about something? "Has she remembered it since? What's the story now?"

Willa's expression darkened. "That's why I wanted to talk to you," she said. "She never seemed to remember it, but I bugged her about it for a week, and eventually she was just like, fine, we went to that house," she said. "Still, I get the feeling she thinks I'm making it up. It's hard to tell, though. It's been, like, two weeks and Izzy's still been acting really weird—she's usually kind of funny and easygoing, but now she's *super* high strung, and gets *really* mad *really* easily. She'll get mad at me when I just act concerned about her—like, hey, maybe you should calm down—and say I'm trying to control her, trying to control her life. Our other friends have noticed the change in her and said something to me too. But I don't know if it's as bad for them."

"Hmm," said Bess.

Owen was looking at his sister, and when she didn't continue, he nudged her again. "Tell them why," he said.

Willa sighed, her downcast expression implying that she didn't want to tell this part. "What's really freaky is . . . she's threatened to hurt me," she said.

"Hurt you?" Bess asked.

"Like, beat me up," Willa explained. "With her fists. Punch me, or kick me."

"Oh," I breathed, surprised. "Has she ever . . . *done* that?"

Willa shook her head. "Never before this—I mean, she would *never* hurt me. We've been best friends forever. We're practically sisters. And even now, it's more of a threat," she said. "Like, 'Stop doing that, stop asking that, stop talking about that, or I'll hit you.' And I usually stop whatever I was doing, because I don't want to know if she'd really do it." She paused, pulling her lips into a tight line and saying in a smaller voice, "She scares me."

I looked at Bess, George, and Ned. I hadn't come to the movies looking for a mystery to solve, but this was really strange—and upsetting. "Have her parents noticed?" I asked. "She's your age, right? She'd interact with them every day."

Willa nodded, her ponytail bobbing. "She does, but I really don't think it's happened in front of them. Even if it did, they'd just probably think it's normal teenage angst or something. No one gives teenagers any credit."

"Ain't that the truth," George said with a frown.

Willa went on, her eyes shining in the dim light, "I'm just really worried about her. No one else seems to see how dangerous she's getting."

"She's acting . . . strangely," Owen spoke up, adding, "She used to be kind of fluffy, goofy, but basically sweet, and now there's a sort of darkness to her. I'm not sure what's going on with her, but something is."

I took in a deep breath. "Strange," I said.

Bess looked from Willa to me, cringing a bit as she asked awkwardly, "I hate to say this, but . . . *could* it just be normal teenage stuff? I mean, there's a lot of . . . things . . . going on when you're Willa's age. People change. It's not exactly unusual for a thirteen- or fourteen-year-old to start acting all emo."

"It's not *emo*," Willa insisted. "It's *dangerous*. The real Izzy would never hurt me, or anyone." She shook her head, frustrated, and went on, "Look, I know how crazy this sounds. I *know*. I've been trying to figure out what to do about it. If I tell her parents, we'll get in trouble for going to the house in the first place—and probably nothing else will happen, because, like I said, they'll call it 'teenage angst.' I can't go to the police— it's not like she's done anything wrong. And even if she had, I don't want to get her sent to jail. I just want her *back*. I want to know that she's okay."

When Willa finished, there was silence for a

moment. She seemed 100 percent sincere—and I couldn't find fault with her concern for her friend. If Izzy was really acting strangely, there was probably more to this case than we knew. Maybe I could help get to the bottom of it.

I sighed. "We've worked haunted-house cases before. There's probably a logical explanation," I said, and I saw Willa's face fall, so I quickly added, "But I guess I can at least check it out."

Just then a horrifying wail started up from the edge of the parking lot.

"*Whoooooooooooooooooooo! Oooooohhh-woooowooooooooo!*"

I let out a scream so loud, if these ghosts were in fact dead, it should have woken them. And I wasn't alone. Bess shrieked and knelt down, like being closer to the ground would save her somehow. Her hand was deep in her purse, digging for her pepper spray, I guess. George laughed nervously, beaming her flashlight in the direction of the wail. Willa screamed, and Owen jumped back. Ned grabbed my hand and started running a couple of steps back toward the street.

But before we could really get anywhere, two teen-agers stepped into the flashlight beam and began cracking up. They were both wearing polo shirts embroidered with the Riverside Cinemas logo. Actually . . . I sort of remembered the guy tearing our tickets.

"Sorry," the girl said, not looking sorry at all. "That was just our fun way of telling you that you need to leave the parking lot immediately. We're closing up."

"Yeah, didn't mean to scare you so bad," the guy added, then cracked up even harder. The girl joined in, and they scurried off toward a white Mini Cooper way at the edge of the parking lot.

Bess turned to me, the blood just beginning to flow back into her face. "You were saying?" she said. "Time to go? *Packed House* awaits."

"I think I just need to go home and go to bed," I muttered, then remembered myself and smiled at Willa. "I'll be in touch, okay? Can I get your contact info?"

"Sure," Willa said, handing me a small piece of paper. "There's my e-mail and Owen's cell. I don't have my own phone yet, but he can find me if you need him to."

"Thanks." I took the paper and put it in my pocket, turning to Ned and my friends. "Now let's get out of here. I think I've had enough thrills and chills to last me a lifetime."

We began walking toward the car, and as we did, I heard Bess murmur under her breath, "I think you just took the wrong case, then."

CHAPTER THREE

The Sound of Evil

DING-DONG-DING-DONG-DING-DONG.

I was startled from my OJ and oatmeal the next morning by someone leaning on our ancient doorbell. Hannah, our housekeeper, glanced toward the front door, then turned to me with a wry smile.

"It's for you," she said, sweeping away my empty oatmeal bowl. "Would you like to let her in?"

Her. There were only three people in my life who would come to my house uninvited and lean on the doorbell at eight a.m., and Hannah had just narrowed it down to two. Would it be the blond, bouncy one

or the dark-haired, sarcastic one? As I approached the door, I could see the answer through the narrow lead-glass window—but she wasn't looking terribly sarcastic today.

Instead, George looked *way jazzed.*

I opened the door a bit warily.

She brushed right past me. "Sorry to come so early," she said. "It's just, I *cannot* stop thinking about Willa's story last night! Do you think the house is really haunted? What do you think happened to that girl? I mean, what other explanation can there be? Right? *Right??*"

I closed the front door, shaking my head. "Did you have coffee?"

George's eyes widened. "*Better,*" she said. "I had an *espresso*. From that place on Third Street where they roast their own beans? I told him I needed some energy, and he said he made it superstrong. *Anyway,* I think I have the perfect Halloween costume for this year. Tell me if you think it's a good one: *Mrs. Furstenberg.*"

She looked at me expectantly, and when I shook my head slightly, her face fell.

"Too soon?" she asked.

"Waaaaaaay too soon," I said, walking past her to lead the way upstairs to my room. "Considering she died under mysterious circumstances and also, she might still be out there haunting kids?" I'd been researching Mrs. Furstenberg's case late into the night and I felt—I dunno—almost *protective* of her.

George followed me up the stairs. "So you *do* think the house is haunted!" she said excitedly. "Nancy Drew, Little Miss Realist! I can't believe it! Willa's story really convinced you, huh? Now you're a believer!"

We'd reached my room, and I sat down on my bed and pulled out my laptop. "I'm not sure what I believe, to be honest with you," I admitted. "I was so tired when we got home last night, but I stayed up late doing Internet research. I just couldn't help myself."

George sat down across from me in the big papasan chair next to the window. "I get it," she said. "I'm fascinated too. Obviously. Anyway, what did you find out?"

I rubbed my eyes and opened up the laptop, scrolling through the different websites I'd left up. "It looks like most of what Willa told us was true: Mrs. Furstenberg died of a heart attack and her son, Henry, is still missing. And the house, since Mrs. Furstenberg left no will and her only heir is missing, was tied up in legal red tape for over a year and left abandoned. The estate was recently given to a distant cousin. The house is for sale, but it's in such bad shape that no one is buying."

"Huh," George said. "Someone does own it, then, technically."

"Right," I said, "but she doesn't live anywhere near River Heights, and doesn't seem super interested in the house itself. That's probably why kids are tromping through it left and right, freaking themselves out."

George nodded, looking thoughtful. I gazed out the window at the neat houses on our street.

"It's strange that Henry took off like that," I said after a few seconds. "Especially if she really died of a heart attack. Why wouldn't he want the house?"

George followed my gaze. "The only thing I can think of," she said, "is that something happened in that house that he doesn't want to think about." She suddenly sat up and shivered like she'd caught a chill. "Sorry. This is all very creepy."

"Yeah," I agreed, glancing back at my computer screen and shutting the laptop. "I *don't* fully believe in ghosts, but it sounds like she had a pretty unhappy life. She and Henry didn't get along, and nobody knew that much about her, which must mean she was lonely. She was found in that little sub-room in the basement, with the door closed. If someone was there when she died, it's almost like they were *hiding* her body."

George raised her eyebrows. "Nancy," she said, "are you going soft? If you don't believe in ghosts, then Mrs. Furstenberg can't be one. Period."

I sighed. "I know, I know," I said. "I just . . . even though I don't believe in ghosts, I thought it would be helpful to consider what her motivation *might* be, if she really were trying to haunt the house. Because maybe whoever really *is* behind this could be using that." I paused. "And thinking about that makes me feel this weird connection to her. Put it this way: if anyone has a good reason to haunt, Mrs. Furstenberg does."

We were quiet for a moment, and then George tried to catch my eye. "So what's next?" she asked. "If I know you, Nancy, you've already got a plan worked out."

"Sort of," I said, remembering the rough plan I'd worked out last night. "I think the first thing we need to do is talk to Izzy."

"The supposedly possessed one?" George nodded slowly. "But the way she's been acting," she said, "at least according to Willa, she might not be open to talking to strangers."

"I agree," I said, putting the laptop back on my desk and standing up. "That's why we'll have to be a little sneaky."

A few hours later, George and I stood waiting outside Izzy and Willa's dance class with a clipboard.

"What do we say again?" George hissed as the front door opened and Willa strode out—followed by a shorter girl with dark curly hair who I could only assume was Izzy.

"Just follow my lead," I hissed back, then raised my voice. "*Excuse me!* Ladies! Are you interested in getting free movie tickets for just a few minutes of your time?"

Willa looked up and smiled, pulling excitedly at Izzy's arm. I'd e-mailed her earlier to let her know George and I would be here to try to get some information from Izzy, and to explain how she could play along. So far, she was doing a great job. Izzy looked more hesitant but allowed Willa to pull her over in our direction.

"How *much* of our time?" Izzy asked a little snootily, glancing behind her. "My mom is coming to pick us up soon, and I can't make her late."

"Barely any time at all," George said, smiling widely.

"A minute tops," I assured them. "We're Tara and Gemma—we work for Spotlight Marketing. We're putting together a trailer for a new horror movie aimed at teenagers, and we wanted to get your input about what scares you."

Willa raised her eyebrows. "Sounds cool," she said, then bumped Izzy with her shoulder. "Come on, Izz, it can't hurt to talk to them. Free movie tickets!"

Izzy looked less sure, but she nodded. "All right. So long as it's fast."

"Okay," I said, picking up my pen and holding it over my clipboard. "Can I ask—which of the following scares you? Zombies, vampires, werewolves, or ghosts?"

"Seriously?" Izzy asked, looking doubtful.

"Zombies," Willa said confidently. "And ghosts, definitely. What about you, Izzy?"

Izzy looked at her friend. "Ghosts, I guess," she said. "The rest of them, meh."

"Zombies don't scare you?" George pressed. "They *eat* your *brains*. Do you watch that zombie show?"

Izzy chuckled. "No, my parents would never let me. But I do really like scary movies."

"Okay," I said, scribbling some pretend notes. "Have you ever had a personal experience with a zombie or ghost?" I turned to Willa.

She laughed nervously. "Seriously? Um . . . no. I guess not. Not that I can prove. Although there *was* this . . ." She looked at Izzy and let out another nervous giggle.

Izzy suddenly turned serious, though. Her eyebrows slanted down over sharp eyes. "What?" she asked.

Willa nudged her friend with her shoulder again. "*You* know," she said, then leaned in to Izzy's ear, dropping her voice to a whisper. I couldn't make out what she was saying anymore.

Izzy's eyes widened. "*That* has nothing to do with this," she said sharply, then pulled away.

"Um, maybe it's sort of, tangentially related?" George said in a hopeful tone. I could tell she was trying to lighten the mood. "We're not going to fact-check you or anything. I mean, this isn't school. It's scary movies!" She laughed.

"Right," I put in smoothly. "It couldn't hurt to just share whatever your friend brought up. Could it?"

Izzy glared at me. "*Why?*" she challenged. There

was something hard in her eyes that hadn't been there before. "So you can put it in your movie?"

"The movie's already made," I said calmly, trying to ignore the weird feeling her hostility was giving me and channel my most professional "marketing associate." "We're just thinking about the trailer. . . . We're not going to publicize what happened to you, honest. This is just a casual chat."

Willa looked nervously at Izzy, who was still staring at me in a not-very-friendly way, and then back at me. "There's this house?" she said hesitantly. "On Heliotrope Lane . . . ?"

I smiled encouragingly and touched my pen to paper, but before Willa could say anything more, Izzy broke in.

At least, she *looked* like Izzy.

"*Shut up and don't you dare tell them anything about it,*" she said, but her voice was suddenly hoarse and five times deeper than it had been before. She reached out and grabbed Willa's arm, squeezing so hard that her knuckles turned white.

Willa let out a startled cry and Izzy let go at once, her eyes scanning the parking lot.

"There's my mom," she said, her voice abruptly returning to normal. "We'd better go—she has a sales call this afternoon."

Before we could stop her, Izzy started walking away, toward a beige SUV where a curly-haired woman waved from the driver's window.

We turned to Willa, stunned.

"Are you okay?" George asked.

Willa was gingerly holding the arm Izzy had grabbed. It had an angry red mark where Izzy's fingers had encircled her wrist.

"I'm okay," she said after a few seconds. "Just . . . startled. You guys heard that, right?" She looked from George to me, her hazel eyes serious.

"We saw it," I confirmed, then lowered my voice. "Willa, are you . . . okay to go with them? We could give you a ride home."

Willa looked at me blankly for a minute, then shook her head. "No. Thank you, but no, I don't want her to think anything's up. And nothing will happen with her mom there." She paused, looking me in the eye. "But you'll do something? Did you get enough information? You'll try to figure this out?"

I nodded. The woman in the SUV was waving to Willa now, and Willa waved back and held up her finger to indicate *just one minute*.

"You have my word, Willa," I said, still feeling a little shaky from the surprise. "I'm going to look into what happened at the house on Heliotrope Lane . . . and we'll figure out what's going on with your friend."

"So what's next?" George asked as we climbed back into my car. "*How* are we going to figure this out?"

I didn't answer for a moment while I concentrated on backing out of the parking space and turning the car onto the road.

"Well," I said finally, "I don't think we exactly endeared ourselves to the victim."

"You can say that again," George scoffed, glancing out at the row of stores we were passing. "I don't think we're going to get much more out of her. In fact, if she sees us approaching her again, I'm not sure what she'd do."

George's features slackened as she stared out at the passing town, seemingly deep in thought. "You heard her voice change?" she asked, and there was an edge of fear in her voice.

"I did," I said. *Much as I'd like to forget it.*

She shook her head. "It didn't sound like her at all. It sounded like . . ."

I shouldn't say this, I told myself. *I should try to reserve judgment. Keep an open mind. Stick to the facts . . .* But I couldn't stop myself.

"Evil," I said softly. "It sounded like a deep, dark hole. Like the absence of any feelings. If evil has a sound . . . that was it."

George looked at me, clearly surprised by my answer. But she nodded. "So what do we do?" she asked after a few seconds.

I sighed. "Well, like you said, we're not going to get much more out of Izzy," I began. "So we're going to have to check out the alleged perpetrator."

George raised her eyebrows. "And that is . . . ?"

"The house on Heliotrope Lane," I said, "and any ghostly inhabitants!"

CHAPTER FOUR

Haunted House

"SO THIS IS WHERE YOU TELL ME THAT ghosts don't exist," I said, peering out my windshield at what was arguably the creepiest house I'd ever seen.

Maybe not *the* creepiest. Maybe that wasn't fair. Maybe it just *seemed* super creepy because I was here alone, in the dark, at the end of Heliotrope Lane, a dead-end street, waiting for Bess and George to show up so we could search a haunted house for a ghost.

"I . . . *am* pretty sure they don't exist," Ned's voice piped up from my phone. He sounded sleepy, probably because it was finals week. He'd told me earlier that he'd stayed up till three a.m. the night before and hadn't woken up until after lunchtime.

"But like, *scientific proof*," I said, leaning closer to the windshield as (I was sure) a light flickered inside the supposedly haunted house. "People's souls have no substance, so they can't take action against living people . . . something like that?"

Ned was silent.

"*Ned!*" I yelled. "Did you fall asleep?"

"Sorry, I'm sorry," he apologized. "Um, ghosts don't exist because . . . be-caaaaaauuse . . ."

"Because it's scientifically impossible?" I prompted. "Ned, have you eaten anything?"

He yawned. "I had some Red Hots?"

"*Real* food?" I urged. "Maybe you should order a pizza. I think it would help your energy level."

"You're probably just experiencing the spiked adrenaline that people get when they're afraid, Nancy," he said. "That doesn't mean ghosts exist. It means . . . you're psyching yourself out."

"Right, right," I agreed, liking this line of thinking.

"Like, I'm seeing things because I've already convinced myself that they're there, like—"

"BOO!"

As a figure suddenly jumped in front of my car, I jumped straight up the air, knocking my head on the ceiling and dropping my phone into the space under the driver's seat.

Outside the car, I heard giggling.

"Nancy?" Ned's voice, barely discernible, called from the floor beneath my seat. "*Nancy? You all right?*"

I rubbed my head, glaring out the windshield at my sort-of-sheepish-looking friend Bess, who was trying to stifle her giggles.

"I'm so sorry," said George, appearing behind her, shaking her head. "I *told* her not to."

I reached a hand under my seat, digging around until I found the phone, and pulled it out.

"Gotta go, Ned," I said. "My fearless associates are here."

I heard a buzzing sound on Ned's side of the

call, followed by muffled voices. "Oh good," he said, "because *my* pizza is here."

"You did order a pizza," I said happily.

"You know what they say about Ned Nickerson," he said, "he's always three steps ahead of his girlfriend, Nancy Drew."

"No one says that."

"Talk to you later. Don't get possessed."

I hung up the phone and, very slowly and carefully, picked up my purse, not making eye contact with my friends.

By the time I got out of the car, they seemed convinced I hated them, which was not that far from the truth.

"*Really* sorry," Bess said, reaching out to touch my shoulder. "It was cruel of me to startle you like that. Is your head okay?"

"Just fine. I'm going to remember this," I said, trying to straighten up into a queenly posture, "and pay you back when you least expect it. Now, are we ready to check out this house?"

"Definitely," said George, nodding like a soldier.

"Not at all," said Bess, nervously twirling a lock of hair around her index finger. "Can I wait in the car? I could be the lookout. I'm a *very* good lookout, you always say that."

"After you just scared the bejesus out of me? Absolutely not." I started walking toward the house, trying to look (and feel) determined. "And I only tell you that to make you feel better when you don't want to come in!"

I knew that was a little mean, but my head still hurt. Also, it was true.

My friends followed, a few steps behind.

Soon we were standing right in front of the supposedly haunted house. Mrs. Furstenberg's house was a small ranch-style home, tucked alone at the end of Heliotrope Lane, which was really more of a cul-de-sac. It had probably been a cute little house while Mrs. Furstenberg had been alive. The shingles were painted a cheery light blue, and there was a low, welcoming porch, perfect for a couple of rocking chairs.

Now, though, the porch was covered with empty cans, plastic bags, and other trash. Animal feces were scattered in a corner. Mold grew near the edges of the windows, and someone had even spray-painted something indistinguishable to the left of the door. I couldn't help wondering what Mrs. Furstenberg would think if she knew what had become of her house.

I jiggled the front door, but a heavy padlock held it closed. I could swear I heard sounds inside, and I stood still for a second, listening.

"What?" George asked behind me.

"Do you hear that?" I asked. It was . . . creaking? Breathing?

"Hear what?" asked Bess.

I shook my head. *Stop psyching yourself out.* "Never mind."

"Let's look for another way in. Maybe there's something in the back," George suggested.

Bess and I nodded in agreement and we all headed for the side of the house.

It looked like the yard hadn't been tended to in

ages; the grass and bushes were totally overgrown. Still, we picked our way around the house. Soon after we turned the corner toward the back, George spotted it: "Is that the broken window?"

She pointed, and we all followed her gaze to a window about four feet from the ground. Most of the glass was missing. An angry-looking holly bush had been planted right in front of it, but clearly many kids before us had forged a path, because there was a spot where the bush had been pushed to the side. In fact, a big rock had been propped in front of the window on the ground.

"A step," Bess said, pointing.

"Yeah, those kids have really got this figured out," I said. "I'm not into trespassing, but this makes our job a lot easier."

George nodded. "You guys ready?" she asked.

I looked the house up and down. Here in the back, there was more graffiti—JULIE WAS HERE, spray-painted at about eye level to the right of the window, and the anarchy symbol, right next to the back door—and the shingles looked grimy even in the dim beam of the flashlight I took out of my purse. Looking up, I could see the roof already starting to sag. And there was a smell—garbage, probably.

The house did something to me—made my heart beat a little faster, made it harder to breathe. But I tried to remember what Ned said (what I had sort of forced him to say) about *adrenaline*. About *psyching myself up*.

"I'm ready," I agreed, hoping to sound determined.

"I'm as ready as I'm going to get," Bess added.

I aimed the flashlight beam through the window, but it caught dust and little else. It was too dark inside—I couldn't make out much. I handed the flashlight to George.

"Here goes nothing," I said, stepping onto the rock and grabbing the window frame. I struggled for a second to pull myself up and through, but soon I was able to get my knee up, and then wiggle through enough to get my legs inside.

I dropped onto a dusty hardwood floor and immediately sneezed.

"Good thinking, Nance," George teased, already stepping up to the window behind me. "Sneeze and let the ghosts know right off that we're here. If they want to possess us, bring it on!"

"Not funny," Bess whined behind her.

I shook my head and shined the flashlight around. It looked like I was in a small living room—or what *had* been a small living room. What little furniture that remained was pretty well trashed. There was still a blue flowered couch, but it was stained and smelly, with rips in the upholstery where fluffy stuffing poked out. Some splintered wood was piled in a corner—what had once been a coffee table, I figured. And across from the couch was a low fireplace, empty and dark. A mantel above it held empty bottles, cans, and chip bags. A large mirror hung over the mantel. Cracks spread outward from a huge punched-in hole in the middle.

I could see my own silhouetted figure behind the flashlight beam in the mirror, and it made me shudder. I was broken into a million pieces.

"Didja find the ghost yet?" George asked eagerly as she climbed through the window and dropped to the floor. Bess climbed through right behind her—though she looked less happy about it.

"No ghost," I confirmed, feeling a teeny bit of relief to have my friends in here with me. "Vandalism: check. Littering: check."

George nodded, looking around the living room. "Seems like the only forces messing with this house right now are human."

"Let's hope so." Bess dropped to the floor after George, frowning as she took in the room. "It smells."

"I'm guessing the trespassers aren't being good little scouts and leaving only footsteps behind," I said.

"What?" Bess looked confused.

"I think Nancy means it stinks because kids are pigs," George said, shining her own flashlight down a hall that extended from the living room to the right. "They leave their trash."

"That was sort of what I was getting at," I said.

"Also, there's probably not a working bathroom in here," George added.

Bess glared at her. "*Ewwww!* Gross, cuz!"

"Sometimes life is gross." George stepped toward the hallway. "It looks a little neater down here. Maybe this leads to the bedrooms?"

She started walking down the hall, and, feeling a little upstaged, I scurried to follow her. But really, I was glad George was here. It was a relief to have someone with me who wasn't scared out of her wits.

The hall *was* neater than the living room, but the ancient striped wallpaper was still ripped off in places, revealing bits of flowered paper beneath. The paper was dark with mold around the tears and near the ceiling.

George sniffed. "Mildew and mold," she said. "That's part of the smell too. We shouldn't stay in here too long. It's not good to breathe in too much mold."

I heard Bess snort from the end of the hallway near the living room. "That's, like, reason one thousand we shouldn't stay here too long."

George shined her flashlight into an open door on the right. "Looks like it used to be a bedroom," she said.

I drew up beside her and peered in. A nearly destroyed mattress with a huge gash in it was leaning in front of a window. On the ground was a wooden bed frame, many of the slats broken or missing. A dresser stood in the corner, but only one drawer hung open—the others were gone.

A torn poster for the movie *Blood Fight* curled up from the wall over the bed.

"This must be the son's room," I whispered. "Henry."

Bess joined us, still not looking happy, and we looked around the room a bit more but didn't find anything else of note.

"All right," I said softly. "Let's move—"

Suddenly there was a loud, scuffling, scratching sound—coming from beneath the broken bed frame.

"AAAAUUGH!" Bess screamed. "Let's get out of—"

But before we could move, the culprit itself

appeared—a huge, matted brown rat! It darted from beneath the bed frame and ran over *George's foot* on its way out the door and down the hallway.

We heard it scuttle away, and then, finally, in the silence, I looked at George. "Are you . . . ?"

She looked at me with an expression of horror. "*No*," she said. "No, I am most definitely not okay. You know what, let's never speak of that again!"

Bess seemed to be struggling to control her breathing. "I want to go home," she whined.

"*You* want to go home?" George asked, eyebrow raised. "*You* need to get out of here now? Who just had a *rat* run over her *foot*?"

Bess shook her head hard, blond hair flying, like she could shake out the memory.

"Let's keep going," George said, stepping back into the hallway. "We have a lot more to check out."

I followed obediently, feeling like George had earned the right to lead. We passed a trashed bathroom and followed the hallway down to the end, where another door opened off to the right. It was closed.

Bess noticed it with alarm. "Maybe we should—"

But George reached out and opened it, without another word. She shined her flashlight inside, and I did the same.

"Mrs. Furstenberg's room," I whispered.

It wasn't in as a bad shape as the other bedroom— possibly because it was farther from the living room. The bare, stained mattress was still *almost* on the bed, spilling off onto the floor on the other side from the door. Two sheer pinkish curtains, one ripped, hung on either side of a window that faced the street. A squat white dresser took up nearly an entire wall, all of its drawers hanging open and empty.

I shined my flashlight toward a darkened doorway on the wall adjacent to the window. I could just make out a shower rod and the pink edge of a bathtub—an en-suite bathroom. I glanced at my friends and gestured, then slowly began making my way over there. It smelled terrible. I stepped inside the doorway and realized it was probably because there was an inch or so of standing water in the bathtub. Something dark and slimy coated the porcelain that was submerged. I groaned and covered my nose with my hand.

"What's up?" George asked.

"Nothing," I said, turning toward her. "It's just some wa—*AAAAAAUUUGGHHH!!*"

There was a mirror on the wall to the right of the door. In the mirror I could see my own face.

And someone else's—drawn, gray, with pupilless black eyes!

"*AUUUUUUGHHH!*"

I was losing it, screaming and too freaked to move, when suddenly George started shaking me.

"Nancy, Nancy, it's okay!" She squeezed my arm and pointed at the mirror. "Look! Nance! It's painted on!"

In her flashlight beam, I could see it—a weird opaque texture on the mirror. *Spray paint.* I took in a deep breath and tried to stop my heart from racing off.

"What kind of sicko spray-paints a face on a mirror?" I asked angrily.

Bess was peeking her head into the bathroom now. "The kind of sicko who thinks sneaking into scary, abandoned houses is fun?" she asked, frowning at the "artwork" on the mirror. "Are you okay, Nancy?"

Breathe. Breathe. "Well, I'm definitely having an adrenaline rush."

Bess looked at me sympathetically. "Maybe we should go now."

"No," I said, even though I really wanted to say *yes*. "We haven't checked out the whole house. There's the basement, we know, which . . ."

Bess's expression darkened. "Which is where Mrs. Furstenberg was found," she finished.

"Right." I led the way out of the bedroom. Bess and George followed.

"The thing is," Bess said as we walked back down the hall to the living room, "I don't want to—I mean—"

"Spit it out, cuz," George said, turning to Bess with a suspicious look. It's easy to forget Bess and George are cousins in addition to being friends—they couldn't be more different.

Bess looked a little guilty. "Maybe I should stay behind," she blurted quickly. "You know—in the living room or something, while you guys check out the basement. I could *keep watch*."

She smiled, clearly proud of her idea, even though it wasn't the first time she'd suggested it while working on a case.

"Oh, here we go again with the 'keep watch' idea. Keep watch for who? Ghosts?" George asked.

"Other trespassers?" I added.

Bess nodded. "All of the above," she said. "I mean, not to be a pessimist or anything, but let's say there *is* something down there, ready to clonk you over the head with a piano."

George stared at her. "There are so many things wrong with that statement," she said warily.

Bess ignored her and continued. "Wouldn't you *want* someone up here, able to go for help?" she asked. "Isn't it better that we don't *all* get clonked?"

George sighed, and we exchanged glances. Hers said something like, *Typical*. Mine said, *No, it's cool*.

"That's a great idea, Bess," I said, turning back to my fair-haired friend, and she smiled as though she hadn't really expected that reaction. "You stay here. Yell if you see anything weird, okay? George and I will find the stairs to the basement and be back in just a few minutes."

I walked toward what looked to be a small kitchen and gestured to George to follow me. The kitchen was modest and kind of out-of-date; it looked like it hadn't been renovated since the seventies or so. It was also filthy and had more spray-painted graffiti on the peeling wallpaper—a name I couldn't quite make out and a weird-looking frowny face.

George walked over to a narrow door next to the stove and opened it. "Here we go," she said, shining her flashlight into the darkness.

A narrow staircase led downward.

We walked to the edge of the stairs and I took in a breath. I knew we had to go down there—and I still didn't *really* believe in ghosts—but something made me want to grab onto the doorframe and refuse to budge. Something about the darkness at the end of George's flashlight beam felt—more than creepy. *Wrong.*

George looked back at me. "Ready?"

I paused for just a moment before nodding. "Ready as I'm going to get."

George went first—for which I was super grateful. As I slowly followed her down the stairs, I tried to remember what Ned had said. *You're just psyching yourself out.* That had to be why this felt so wrong. The adrenaline spike I'd had after the scare in the bathroom had to explain why my arm was shaking so badly the flashlight beam wiggled all over.

George reached the bottom of the steps and moved to the side, shining her light around the space. We were in one large room, clearly used for storage. It was darker down here than on the first floor; small, one-foot-tall windows set into the foundation at ground level would let in only the tiniest amount of light from outdoors—almost none at this hour—and besides, many of them were blocked by plants on the other side. Tools hung on the wall next to the stairs. Shelves lined two walls, and I could make out a beat-up-looking washing machine and dryer. Many of the shelves were empty, and I wondered if they had been when Mrs. Furstenberg died, or whether the kids who'd been trespassing through the house had helped themselves to her belongings. *That would make me mad enough to haunt,* I thought, then chastised myself: *Not that ghosts are real!*

"Do you see anything?" George asked. "Isn't there a smaller room down here? Willa said she found Izzy in a smaller room. . . ."

"The room where Mrs. Furstenberg's body was found," I added. "Yeah. That's what I thought. But I don't see anything."

George's brows furrowed as she shined her light along the ceiling. Her beam made a straight line across the wall where the washing machine was, then made a sharp right, then moved along the following wall, then . . .

"There!" I said. "See? The wall comes in, but it doesn't extend all the way to the end of the house. There's a room or a closet or something over there."

George nodded. "You're right."

Slowly, holding my flashlight beam in front of me, I led the way over to the place where the wall seemed to be hiding something. It was a small space, less than eight feet long.

When I got closer, I shined my flashlight along one wall—then around the corner . . .

"There!" said George.

A heavy metal door painted black led into the cornered-off space.

A chill ran down my spine. "That has to be where they found her body," I whispered.

"But who closed it?" George asked. "If Willa found Izzy in there . . . and no one lives here . . ."

I shivered. I didn't like thinking about this. Either someone who was trespassing in the house had reason to close it, or . . . *someone who's not alive is keeping us out?* "Unless there's another room?" I asked, quickly scanning the walls again with my flashlight.

"There's not," George said. "This has to be it."

I sighed, then looked at my friend. "So I guess . . ."

". . . we should at least try the door," George said,

though she looked about as eager as I felt, which is to say: not very.

I was shaking now. I tried to hide it, to hold my flashlight still, but every nerve in my body seemed to be warning me *not* to try to open this door. Instead I wanted to flee. I wanted to go screaming up the stairs and grab Bess and all of us plow back through the broken window to run across the lawn and *away* from this house.

That's when I thought . . . *What if Mrs. Furstenberg's ghost just wishes we would all go away and leave her alone? Maybe she's mad her house has become a sort of tourist attraction. Maybe whatever she did to Izzy was a warning . . . and if we open this door, we'll become part of that warning too.*

"Come on, Nancy," George said, placing her hand firmly around the doorknob. "Put your hand over mine."

I held out my shaking hand. I did what I'd been told, even though I *really* didn't want to.

"Okay," George said. "One . . . two . . . three . . ."

Together, we tried to twist the doorknob. But nothing happened. The door wouldn't budge.

George and I looked at each other in surprise. "What's—" I began.

And a woman's horrific scream cut through the air.

CHAPTER FIVE

Intruders

I SUPPOSE IT DOESN'T MAKE A *TON* OF SENSE to scream when you hear a scream, but that's what we did.

"AUUUUUUUUUGHHHH!"

George and I were so stunned, so freaked out, that it took us a moment to realize that the door was still closed and we were still alone in the basement.

The scream was coming from upstairs.

"Bess!" George cried, her dark eyes wide with worry. "Did something happen to her?"

"Let's go," I said, but by that time George was

already across the basement and mounting the narrow staircase. I bolted behind her, and we ran up to the kitchen as fast as we possibly could.

"Bess?" George shouted when we emerged into the kitchen. "What happened? Are you okay?!"

"I'm in here." Bess's voice floated in from the living room. After the intensity of her scream, she sounded eerily calm. I couldn't help thinking of what Willa had told us about Izzy—how quiet she was after Willa found her in the basement.

My breath caught in my chest. *What's going on?*

We rushed into the living room, where Bess was standing straight and calm. I was so relieved to see her that it took me a moment to realize she wasn't the only person in the room. She was facing off with three teenage boys.

"Hey!" George cried, frowning at one of the three new intruders. "We know you!"

"*Owen!*" I cried, because I realized who he was. Owen. Willa's brother, who we'd met at the movie theater. Owen, who hadn't really wanted to be there—but did back up his sister's claims about Izzy.

"What are *you* doing here, Owen?" George demanded. "What did you do to freak out my cousin?"

Owen's scowl looked less than apologetic, but then he seemed to undergo a change, standing up straight and softening his features. "Look, I'm sorry we scared you," he said to Bess. "I forgot that we met before, and I didn't know anyone was in here. This is Dev and Wyatt, my friends."

Bess, George, and I all nodded at the boys. "Hi," I said. "And what exactly are you all doing here?"

The boys looked a little embarrassed—especially Owen. "Well, ah, I guess rumors are going around school now about what happened to Izzy," he said. "A lot of people—including my friends—wanted to check out the haunted house."

Bess was frowning. "That's interesting, isn't it?" she asked, a skeptical look on her face.

"What do you mean?" Owen asked.

She shrugged. "Just that word is spreading around your school about what happened to your sister's friend . . . and aren't you the only one at your school who knows Izzy? Isn't she in middle school?"

Good point. I shot Bess an appreciative glance, silently thanking her for her quick thinking.

Dev and Wyatt chuckled nervously, and Wyatt glanced sideways at Owen and coughed over the word "Busted!"

Owen grinned sheepishly and looked down at the floor. "I mean . . . okay. I might have said something to my friends about Izzy." He looked up, glancing from Bess, to George, to me. "There's nothing wrong with that, is there? It's super weird. *I* don't believe in ghosts personally, but Dev watches all those real-life ghost hunter docs. So I brought him and Wyatt to check it out."

I raised my eyebrows. "You don't believe in ghosts personally, so you hire us to check out the haunted house and then turn it into a tourist attraction?"

Wyatt laughed loudly. "*Dude,*" he said, cuffing Owen on the arm. "I don't know what you did to this girl, but she's *mad.*"

But Owen was looking less amused, even defensive now. "There's nothing wrong with my bringing friends here," he said. "Not any more wrong than you being here already. And besides, Willa hired you—not me."

Hmmmm. "Okay. But you were there."

He looked up at me, hostility flashing in his eyes. "*I* didn't hire you. I wouldn't have."

"Is that so?" I asked evenly. "You don't have a lot of faith in my abilities, huh?"

He shook his head. "That's not it. I don't know anything about you." He paused, looking around the trashed living room. "I just don't think there's a mystery to solve here."

George placed a hand on her hip. "But you just said you don't believe in ghosts," she pointed out.

"That's right," Owen said.

Bess let out a frustrated sigh. "So if it's not ghosts . . . what do *you* think is happening with Izzy?"

Owen lifted his chin and shrugged. "Isn't it obvious?" he asked. "She's playing my sister. None of this is real."

That surprised me, but I tried to keep my face neutral as I asked, "Why would she do that?" When Owen looked surprised by the question, I added, "They're best friends, right? And it's obviously making Willa really upset."

Owen kept his chin high, almost challenging. "I don't know," he said, finally looking away, toward his friends. "I just know she's faking."

I'd been paying so much attention to Owen that I didn't notice that Wyatt and Dev had started moving around the room, checking out all the furniture and decorations. "Oops!" Wyatt called now, followed by a huge *crash!* I turned around and saw that he'd knocked an old framed art print off the wall, and the glass had shattered in the frame.

"Hey!" George yelled, frowning.

"What's the big deal?" Dev asked, holding his arms wide. "This place is trashed anyway. It's not like anyone *lives* here—well, not anyone *alive*." He snickered.

Bess looked from his face down to the level of his waist. "Is that spray paint?" she asked.

Sure enough. When Dev had spread his arms, his jacket had parted to reveal cans of spray paint in each of his pants pockets. "Uh . . . ," he stammered, quickly pulling his jacket to cover them.

I fished my phone out of my pocket and held it up. "*All right*," I said. "Look, it's been fun, guys, but the fact is, we're all trespassing here. And I think we should all leave now—or else I'll call the cops."

Wyatt and Dev immediately started whining, but Owen looked right at me with a look of barely contained fury.

"Who put *you* in charge?" he asked.

"I guess no one did," I said, irritated, "but I have a phone with a 911 button and a pretty good relationship with the River Heights PD. If I call and they show up, who do you think they're going to believe—me or you?"

Owen scowled at me but turned, shook his head, and finally said to his friends, "We'd better go, guys. Sorry." He turned back and glared at me again. "We can come back another time, when Princess Narc isn't here."

I couldn't help smirking at that. *"Princess* Narc," I said, nodding my approval. "Most people just call me Narc, or Miss Narc, or Narcypants. Thanks for the promotion."

Owen grunted and turned back toward the broken window. He climbed out, followed by his friends. Bess and George looked at me.

"Are we really done here?" George asked, looking around with an almost wistful expression.

"For now," I said. "I think we saw everything there is to see."

"Except the locked room," she said in a low voice.

I nodded. "Except that. But now isn't the time."

We all climbed back through the window, then circled around to the front of the house, where the boys had collected near an old Honda Civic. There was an awkward moment where they just watched us watching them.

"Aren't you going to go?" I asked finally.

Owen scowled again. "Come on, guys," he said, pulling out a set of car keys and walking around to the driver's-side door of the Civic. I heard the click of the doors unlocking, and then Wyatt and Dev reluctantly got into the front passenger seat and back seat, respectively. Three petulant faces watched me as Owen started up the ignition. After a few minutes, the car pulled into the street.

Bess, George, and I all watched as Owen drove to the end of Heliotrope Lane and then turned onto Elm Street. George started to say something, but I held up my hand to stop her as I listened to the engine noise dwindling in the distance.

After a minute or so, when the car didn't reappear, I nodded. "Shall we go?"

"Please," Bess said. "I think I'm good on haunted houses for the night."

George raised an eyebrow at me. "Did you learn anything useful, Nancy?"

I shook my head. "I don't . . . think so. I was freaked out in there, I'll admit, but I don't think we found any evidence that the place is *haunted*. Unsettling, yes. Being torn apart by curious trespassers, yes."

George agreed. "If I were Mrs. Furstenberg and I saw what was happening to my house, I might be mad enough to haunt it. But I don't think we saw a ghost in there."

Bess shuddered. "Thank heavens."

We walked over to our parked cars, and just as I pulled out my key fob and pushed the unlock button, I heard Bess's gasp.

"Oh no!"

I turned around and saw Bess holding her hand in front of her face, looking crestfallen.

"What happened?" asked George. "Did you get a cut or something?"

Bess shook her head. "Worse," she said. "My charm bracelet is gone."

George groaned. "The one your dad gave you?" she asked. Bess nodded. "You wore it tonight?" George asked.

"I wear it all the time," Bess said innocently. "I just didn't think to take it off. Anyway, it must have fallen off in the house, guys. I can't leave without it.

But I think it might be in one of the bedrooms—I sort of remember hearing a clink, but there were so many weird noises, I didn't think much about it."

I took in a breath, glancing back at the dark, creepy house. *I don't want to go back in there.* My stomach clenched at the very thought.

But I also knew I was being a wuss. We hadn't found any evidence of ghosts in the house. And I couldn't exactly ask Bess to give up a beloved gift just because she'd dropped it in a scary place. She was my friend, and I owed it to her to help find it.

"Okay," I said, locking my car again. "Let's go back in."

The living room of the house was just as we'd left it—except it seemed even darker now after being outside. I looked at the broken art print on the floor and cringed. *How long before everything in here is completely wrecked?*

Bess hesitantly walked down the hall to the bedrooms, peeking her head into the first. George and I followed a few steps behind.

"Look out," George said. "Spoiler: there's a rat in there."

Bess suddenly let out a gasp and sprinted into the room, grabbing something from the floor near the mattress. "Here it is, guys," she said. She wrapped the chain around her wrist and quickly clasped it. "*Thank goodness. Okay, now we can go.*"

But as we all went back to the living room, I heard it.

"Hold on," I whispered, holding up my hand for everyone to stop and be quiet.

A low sound—almost like a rumbling.

It was coming from the basement.

I could hear my friends' ragged breath as we all struggled to make out the sound. At first there was silence—and I wondered if I was hearing things, getting tired and loopy—but then I heard it again.

Not rumbling. *Moaning.*

"*Ohhhhhhhhh . . .*"

Ice prickled in my veins as I turned to face my friends, who looked just as horrified as I was.

Is somebody down there? Or . . . something that used to be somebody?

Then, suddenly, we were all knocked off our feet by a sudden, much larger sound—*WOOWOOWOOWOOWOO!*

Police sirens!

"Oh *no*," George groaned, as flashing lights reflected off the walls.

A voice began speaking through a megaphone. "We know you're in there. You're trespassing on private property. Come out with your hands up. . . ."

My friends and I all did as the police said. Soon we were lined up on the front lawn, blinded by high-powered flashlights as two officers looked us up and down, their lips pursed with disgust.

One of them was Officer Faith Fernandez. "We've gotten reports of kids running around the abandoned house," she said. "But—*Nancy Drew*? Is that you?"

I nodded. "Uh," I said, not sure where to start. "Maybe it won't surprise you, but . . ."

". . . you're working on a case?" Officer Hernandez's

partner, Officer Collins, filled in. He didn't exactly look impressed.

"Yeah," I admitted.

Officer Fernandez sighed. "Honestly . . . ," she muttered, looking behind us at the abandoned house. "Well, listen, ladies. I think you'd better come with us."

She unclipped a pair of handcuffs from her belt and held them up, glinting, in the light.

CHAPTER SIX

Who Knows You Best?

"I'M STARVING," BESS MURMURED, SQUIRMING in a hard plastic chair at the River Heights Police Station.

George frowned at her. "Bess," she said, "that is *literally* the least of our problems right now."

"On the bright side, we're not being charged with anything," I piped up, feeling sincerely grateful for the officers' mercy. Though they *had* given us quite a lecture about the dangers of trespassing, the stupidity of the whole fascination with the Furstenberg house, and the fact that there was nothing wrong with Izzy besides *being a teenager*, which was the *worst* (chortle).

When I tried to press Officers Fernandez and Collins about what happened to Mrs. Furstenberg, they said it was probably just an accident, "but people do love being morbid." For some reason, that wasn't much comfort. They confirmed that they had spent a year looking for Mrs. Furstenberg's son, Henry, but that they hadn't had much luck, and now that the estate had been passed on to a cousin, the case was considered closed.

As Bess continued to moan about her hunger, I heard a familiar voice from the reception desk. ". . . my daughter, Nancy?"

"Shhhh," I hissed at Bess.

"Of course, Mr. Drew," the receptionist said smoothly. "You'll just need to sign these papers. I'll go get her."

I shot an apologetic smile at Bess and George for being the first one picked up, but they just smiled back and waved me on. When the receptionist came in, I stood and followed her, as instructed, to the lobby. My dad was standing there, straight and tall, holding his coat with an unreadable expression.

"Hey," I said nervously, hoping for a smile.

"Hey," he replied, his serious face dissolving as he smiled back.

"Look, I'm not foolish enough to think that you'd stop investigating a case just because the police picked you up," Dad was saying as we turned onto Elm Street, "but I want you to be careful. I know you have a good head on your shoulders, but I don't want you taking any unnecessary risks."

"I know, Dad." I had to admit, I was feeling a little sheepish about the double trespassing I'd committed earlier that night—but how else was I supposed to find out the truth? "It's just—I know it's not a ghost. So what's going on?"

Dad shrugged as he turned onto Heliotrope Lane. "I have learned in my law work that people are endlessly creative about finding new ways to drive each other crazy," he said in an even tone.

"So you think Owen's right?" I asked. "Izzy's faking it?"

"I think it's worth looking into that possibility," he said.

"But how?" I asked. Dad was pulling up to the abandoned house at the end of the lane now, and I couldn't bring myself to even look at it. He stopped near my parked car. "How do you prove someone is acting strange on purpose?" I pressed further.

"I suppose you try to talk to the people who know them best."

"But who knows Izzy best?" I asked, seriously wondering. *Willa is her best friend, and she can't figure it out.* I pulled my key fob out of my pocket again and unlocked my car's doors. The car honked as though happy to be reclaimed.

Dad put his car in park and reached into his coat pocket. "I don't know," he said. "Who knows someone best?" He pulled his hand out of his pocket and handed me a small Ziploc bag—stuffed with two of Hannah's famous oatmeal raisin cookies. I reached for it eagerly, and he smiled. "I thought you might be hungry."

"Oh gosh, Dad, thank you." I ripped into the bag and shoved a cookie in my mouth. *Heaven. How did he know this was exactly what I needed to cheer me up?*

"It's just a house, Nancy." I glanced up and saw my dad staring out the window at the Furstenberg house.

"I know." I hugged Dad, opened the door, and climbed out, dashing the ten feet or so to my car and opening the driver's-side door.

Just as he began to pull away, a chill went down my spine. I immediately turned and looked at the house. It felt like my gaze was being pulled there by a magnet. Nothing looked out of place, but I had the strong, distinct feeling that I was being watched.

Mrs. Furstenberg?

Hands shaking, I slid into the driver's seat and slammed the door behind me, quickly locking the doors. Still staring at the house, I turned the key in the ignition and threw my seat belt on, then flicked on the headlights. Without hesitating, I put the car into reverse and looked through the back window, ready to get away from Heliotrope Lane.

But when I looked over one last time, in the darkness, I could swear I saw something—and my blood went cold.

In the glow of the car taillights, a pair of eyes reflected back from a basement window.

"Hey, Nancy." Willa grinned at me as she walked into the Coffee Cabin, a coffee shop not that far from River Heights Middle School. I'd e-mailed her to meet me here after school on Monday, and she was right on time. Her long hair was woven into a braid today that hung over her shoulder. "What's up? Oh, remind me I have something to show you."

I put down my hot chocolate and pushed a plate of butter cookies across the table to Willa. "Okay. Here, take one. Well . . . you probably already know from Owen. I went to the house on Heliotrope Lane on Saturday night."

Willa grabbed a cookie and nodded seriously. "What happened?"

"Well . . . nothing, really," I said honestly. "At least, nothing that gave me answers about Izzy. We *did* run into Owen, who was taking his friends on some kind of tour."

Willa grimaced. "Yeah, he mentioned that. I'm sorry. He's an idiot."

I took a sip of hot chocolate. "He said he thinks Izzy is faking it," I said slowly.

Willa had been taking a bite of her cookie, and she paused, startled, before quickly swallowing the bite in her mouth. "Um, yeah," she said. "He told me after we talked to you. . . . I guess he doesn't agree with me that something's up with her. But think, who knows her better? Owen . . . or me?"

"It sounds like you," I said.

"Right." Willa smiled and finished her cookie.

"It's just . . ." I looked out the window at the middle school kids passing by. They were all smiling and chatting, heaving backpacks up on their shoulders. *Could any of them be capable of faking ghost possession, or worse?* "I believe you, Willa, but I think I need to talk to someone *else* who knows Izzy really well. Her parents."

Willa's face turned pale, and she shook her head, her braid whipping back and forth. "No—Nancy, please."

"But maybe there's a perfectly rational explanation, Willa," I said softly. "Maybe there's something going on in Izzy's life that you just don't know about. . . ."

Willa groaned. "No, she tells me everything, Nancy. She'd tell me *before* she told her parents. Don't you get that? We've been best friends since we were five."

I sighed. "I just really think it would help to talk to them."

"*No*," she insisted. "Please, Nancy. As soon as you contact her parents, Izzy will find out that I told you about her weird behavior, and then . . ."

"Then what?" I asked.

Willa's eyes unfocused, and she shuddered. "I don't know," she said, looking at me angrily. "That's why I contacted you. *She scares me.* I don't know what she'll do if she knows I told someone. She gets so angry now!"

"But . . . what if her parents didn't tell her?" I suggested. "What if I asked them not to?"

Willa looked doubtful. "I mean, you could try. But Izzy's parents are like, *crazy* strict—she would be grounded for life if they knew we had snuck into the haunted house! I don't think they'd be super concerned about how *you* wanted them to react."

I nodded. *Parents.* "But maybe there's some way . . . ," I began, then trailed off, at a loss.

"I don't think so—not without tipping off Izzy," Willa said. "Look, is there anything else you can do? I'm really worried about my friend—that's why I got in touch with you in the first place."

I looked down into my mug, then out at the street. *I need a way to make sure that what's happening to Izzy is real.* Then it occurred to me—with all the kids traipsing in and out of the house on Heliotrope Lane every night, if something really *was* happening in there . . . wouldn't there be more than one victim?

"I have an idea!" Willa said suddenly, pointing her

finger into the air. "It's what I wanted to remember to show you. May I borrow your phone?" I handed my phone to her, and she went on, "Owen said something about a kid at his school. It's new. Like, it happened to him recently."

Wow. It's like she was a mind reader!

"A high school student?" I prompted, wondering if it might be someone I knew.

"Yeah, a junior . . . his name is Gavin," Willa said. "Gavin Yoo."

Gavin Yoo. I was vaguely familiar with the kid— maybe we'd once had a class together? But I could only call up a vague picture. I didn't know him well.

"The thing I want to show you is," Willa went on, scrolling through my phone, "Owen sent me a video. Let me see if I can find it. . . . Oh! Here."

She pulled up a video and showed me the screen.

"I don't want to talk about it," a tall, short-haired Asian boy was saying, sitting at a table in what looked like the cafeteria in RHHS. He looked down, blushing slightly. He was wearing a varsity baseball jacket.

"Oh, come on, Gavin," a male voice off-camera teased. "Are you afraid *Lila* might find out?"

Gavin's blush deepened. "Shut up," he muttered, smiling down into his can of soda. "Let's talk about something else. Did you guys watch the end of *Bot Kingdom* yet?"

"No," the voice off-camera said. "So let's talk about something *else* creepy."

"Yeah," another male voice chimed in. "Let's talk about what happened the other night."

Suddenly Gavin looked straight at the camera, and something immediately changed in his face. All the levity, all the bashfulness disappeared, and he stared into the lens with a look of serious disapproval—even dread.

"Let's not," he said, and his voice was different, deeper.

"Yeah," the other off-camera voice chimed in, laughing, clearly not picking up on how serious Gavin looked. "Let's talk about what happened to you at the house on Heliotrope Lane."

At the word "house," Gavin's face changed even more. The muscles in his jaw seemed to go slack, and he pitched his face downward, peering up at the camera through dark, furious eyes. I felt a chill go down my spine.

"I told you I don't want to talk about it," he said. Except it wasn't really his voice anymore. It was deeper again, but this time, it was like he had gargled with rocks or drunk acid. The sound coming out of him was angry, dark, ugly. . . .

"He sounds like a demon," I whispered to Willa. "Like Izzy sounded when she was angry with us outside the dance studio."

Willa nodded. In the video, Gavin continued growling, *"It's none of your business. Don't make me hurt you."* Then he raised his hand in a clawlike shape above the edge of the table.

"Oh, come on," the off-camera voice chided again, still not sounding like he understood how serious this was becoming. "I just want to know—"

But then I jumped as I watched Gavin lunge

forward, knocking the camera to the ground.

There was a crash, and then the video winked out.

I put the phone down and then looked up at Willa. "This is serious. Does he know Izzy at all?" I asked.

She shrugged. "I don't think so. I definitely don't know him," she said. "I just found out about him before school today."

I frowned. "Why is there a video?" I asked. "Does Gavin know about it? Who took it?"

Willa glanced down at the phone as the screen turned black, then up at me. "I'm not really sure," she said. "Owen said one of his friends took it. I think when they started taking the video, they didn't realize how serious it was. But now they're really worried."

I pressed the wake button on the phone. The video had stopped on a freaky image of Gavin's furious face. Willa looked at it a moment before continuing.

"Like me and Izzy," she said, "Gavin's friends are scared to tell anyone because they're worried about getting in trouble for sneaking into the house. They know it was trespassing."

I pressed play and we both watched the video again. This time I was even more struck by the difference between Gavin's sweet, embarrassed demeanor at the beginning and the angry, vengeful force that seemed to emanate from him at the end. *But is the transformation real?* I couldn't know, because I knew so little about Gavin.

"Maybe I can talk to him," I said slowly, pushing the phone back over to Willa. "If he asks, I can say I got his name from Owen."

A wave of relief seemed to wash over Willa's face. "Thank you, Nancy," she said. "I really appreciate your not talking to Izzy's parents."

I nodded. "For now. I can't promise I still won't need to," I said.

"That's okay," Willa said, smiling. "As long as you keep working on the case. I really want to understand what's happening to Izzy."

Me too, I thought, remembering Izzy's fury outside

her dance lesson. *For you—and for Izzy.*

Then my mind went back to the house on Heliotrope Lane—and the eyes I'd felt watching me from the basement window.

And for Mrs. Furstenberg, I added mentally.

CHAPTER SEVEN

Another Victim

THE COOL WIND SEEMED TO PIERCE through my fleece jacket and hug my bones as I waited in the parking lot for Gavin Yoo. It was the day after I'd met with Willa, and unusually chilly for spring. I checked my phone and confirmed that baseball practice should be letting out any minute.

I was glad. It was cold, I was tired, and it was nearly time to go home for dinner. Hannah was making her famous pork chops; I'd deduced this by texting my dad.

But Gavin Yoo seemed to be taking his sweet time. After a few minutes, I began seeing his teammates walking from the baseball field to their cars, making their good-byes, climbing in and driving off. One by one, the cars in the parking lot dwindled. A few guys cast curious glances my way, but no one said anything.

I checked my watch. It had been half an hour since I'd arrived, and I was officially late for dinner.

TELL HANNAH I'M SORRY, I texted Dad. BUT I'M STARVING AND I'LL BE THERE ASAP.

Then another ten minutes ticked by with no sign of Gavin. I was pretty sure all his teammates had left—and he hadn't been with any of them. Only two cars were left—mine and Gavin's.

I stared in the direction of the baseball field, but I couldn't make out any figures on the grass.

Maybe I missed him?

I wasn't sure how. Maybe he got a ride home with a teammate while I was looking the other way?

But then why is his car still here?

It was weird. Why would he get a ride home with someone else if his car was right here?

But where else could he be?

I sighed and checked my phone again. Now it had been twenty minutes since I'd texted Dad—who'd texted back IT'S OKAY, MORE PORK CHOPS FOR ME—and I'd been standing in this parking lot for nearly an hour. It was getting dark. I shivered inside my fleece. *Maybe Gavin's car isn't working, or else he decided to sleep over at a friend's? Either way, I can't stand here all night.*

I was starving. And freezing. *It's time to go home.*

When I'd arrived, the parking lot had been much fuller, so I'd parked way over by the high school gym. I turned in that direction now and began hustling along, pulling my car keys out of my pocket and fingering the unlock button. I couldn't wait to get inside and blast the heat. It was one of those last-gasp-of-winter days where it's been warm for a long time, and then suddenly you get this chilly weather back. . . .

A hand reached out from behind me and grabbed my shoulder.

"Looking for me?"

All the breath left my body in one gasp. It was the

same gargled-with-rocks, evil voice from the video I'd watched with Willa.

Don't show him you're scared, a tiny voice whispered inside me. So I tried to pull myself up to my full height and hide the fear from my face as I turned around to face Gavin Yoo.

It took me a minute to make him out in the dwindling light. Still, I stifled a scream at the sight of him. His expression and bearing were completely different from the shy athlete I'd seen at the beginning of the video. His face was cast downward, and each muscle in his jaw seemed to be clenched tight. Again, he was staring at me from beneath an angry brow. *He looks like a feral animal,* I thought.

"Hi," I said, hoping he couldn't tell that I was struggling to keep my voice even. "I *was* looking for you, actually. I'm Nancy Drew—"

"*We all know who you are, Nancy,*" Gavin hissed. In addition to being deep and garbled, Gavin's voice almost had a skittering tone to it—like there were bugs in his chest. *Like something died inside him,* I thought.

"We all know what you're trying to do." He smiled, and the light from the streetlights seemed to catch his canines, giving him a kind of fanged look. *"And we won't let that happen, understand?"*

He lunged forward, and I couldn't keep my cool anymore—I shrieked and jumped back. But instead of advancing, this strange version of Gavin threw back his head and let out a high, terrifying cackle. When I paused, staring in confusion, he suddenly moved toward me and shoved me. The force was surprising, sending me toppling to the ground. I opened my mouth to scream but couldn't draw a breath.

Gavin stood over me, leering. *"Mind your own business, Nancy Drew,"* he said, his words dripping with contempt, *"or you'll be next."*

Then, just as quickly as he'd appeared, he disappeared into the darkness.

I shakily got to my feet and pulled out my phone. The whole confrontation with Gavin had taken a whopping three minutes. And there was a new text from my dad: BREAKING NEWS: APPLE PIE!!!!

My dad does love a good apple pie.

Still, I was still trembling as I walked the rest of the way to my car. My legs felt like spaghetti. And as hard as I tried, I couldn't catch my breath. I felt weak and jumpy—like any minute, someone might try to grab me from another side.

He *could*, I supposed. I hadn't seen where he'd gone. . . .

Finally I reached my car and unlocked it, jumping into the driver's seat and locking the doors around me.

What *was* that? And who was he talking about when he said *we* . . . as in *we won't let that happen*?

Gavin and Izzy? Or Gavin and Izzy and . . . *someone else*?

"I have to go back there."

I was at George's house now, having called Bess and George to meet me there as soon as I was done with dinner. I'd told them both about my experience with Gavin Yoo, and they seemed as shaken by my story as I felt.

"Go back *where*?" Bess asked. "Nancy, if this experience teaches us anything, it's that you can't go confronting these people alone anymore. If you want to try to talk to Gavin again, take me or George with you."

"Not Gavin. I'm not talking about confronting Gavin."

"Where, then?" George asked, one eyebrow raised. When I met her eye, I could tell she understood immediately. "Oh no," she muttered.

I looked at Bess. "I have to go back to the house on Heliotrope Lane," I said as she gasped, "and try to find out once and for all what's going on there. Maybe I didn't stay long enough last time. Maybe—"

Bess shook her head furiously. "No," she said. "Nancy, no, no, no, no."

"Why not?" I said. "I know it didn't work out well last time. But—"

"I just don't think we'll *find* anything," Bess interrupted, nervously fingering George's fuzzy bedspread. "I mean, didn't we *do* that already? We searched the house. We didn't find anything unusual."

"Maybe we weren't looking in the right places," I said, glancing at George. "I mean . . . there was that room in the basement. . . ."

"Room in the basement?" Bess asked, her forehead crinkling as she looked from George to me.

"Bess, the door to the room in the basement where Mrs. Furstenberg's body was found was closed, and we couldn't get it open. It must have been locked from the inside."

Bess looked back and forth from George to me. "But who would have locked that door? And why?"

"Someone who doesn't want anyone finding out what's inside," I speculated. "Which makes me think there's more to see. I also . . ." I paused, not sure whether I wanted to continue.

"What?" George looked at me expectantly.

I shook my head. "Later, when I went back to get my car . . . When my dad dropped me off . . . I felt like . . . I know this sounds crazy . . . but like something was *watching* me." I looked down at the floor, then back at my friends.

They were both staring at me, openmouthed.

"When I drove away," I added, "I thought my headlights reflected off . . . a pair of eyes. In the basement."

Bess let out a huge breath and said, "Hoo boy. Okay." She went on resolutely, "Listen, guys, I need to be honest with you right now. I can't go back there."

George looked at her cousin, her expression disappointed. "Why *not*?"

Bess ran her hand over her face. "I know this is going to sound crazy. I know you're going to be like, 'Oh, spooked-out Bess, always getting freaked by the silliest things.' But"—she stopped for a moment, then met my eyes—"I just can't go back there, Nancy. I know we didn't find anything weird. But something about that place . . . it felt *evil* to me."

Bess's words should have upset me, but they didn't. Instead, when she spoke I felt that weird sense of relief that I often do when someone says what I'm feeling so I don't have to.

Because Bess was right, in a way. I felt it deep in my soul.

"I'll go back with you, Nancy," George said, looking serious, but she didn't exactly sound eager to do it. "If you want to. But remember . . . we got rounded up by the police last time." She paused. "Maybe we should wait until we have a clearer game plan?" she asked. "Maybe we all need to think about this some more."

I nodded. George was right—I didn't know what I expected to find in the Furstenberg house, anyway. I didn't know what I was looking for.

I just knew there was *something*.

Something about this whole thing was bothering me . . . and I couldn't figure out what it was.

Later that night, I jumped up in my bed, startled from sleep. As I stared out the window at the moon, it came to me—what had been bothering me about Willa's case.

"That's it!" I shouted.

CHAPTER EIGHT

Confrontation

THE NEXT AFTERNOON FOUND ME BACK in the RHHS parking lot—but this time, waiting for a different person. I pulled my fleece close around me, watching the clouds roll in over the baseball field and wondering when I would find out the truth about what had happened to Izzy and Gavin. *Soon, I hope,* I thought.

"Hey!" I cried, watching my mark walk from the main building toward a car.

Owen turned and looked at me with an expression like I was something he'd scraped off the bottom of his shoe. "You're out of luck," he called with a sneer. "I'm not picking up Willa today. You'll have to find some other way to get in touch with her."

I advanced toward him, shaking my head. "No," I said, "it's *you* I want to talk to."

Owen grimaced. "Can we at least get in my car?" he asked, pulling his arms around himself. "It's getting cold, and I don't have a jacket."

I noticed he was just wearing a long-sleeved T-shirt, black with some kind of heavy metal band logo. "Fine," I said. "But I'm leaving my door open." I've worked too many cases where a friend suddenly turned enemy after I'd climbed into their car.

But Owen just rolled his eyes. "Whatever."

He led me to the same battered Honda Civic I'd seen at the Furstenberg house the night he'd shown up with Dev and Wyatt. He opened the driver's door, leaned over, and unlocked the passenger side by hand. I walked over to that side and climbed in, leaving the door open wide and one foot on the parking lot ground.

He was already settled in the driver's seat. He sighed as I put my purse on the floor in front of me.

"All right, shoot," he said, looking away and out the front windshield toward the baseball field. "I don't have all day."

I stared at him for a moment, waiting for him to turn his attention back to me. I wanted him to know I was taking this conversation seriously.

"*What?*" he asked, looking openly annoyed now.

"Do you remember what you told me at the haunted house—that you don't believe in ghosts?" I asked.

"Sure," he said.

"So that means you think Izzy is faking it," I went on.

He nodded abruptly. "Yup," he said, raising his eyebrows as if to add, *Duh.* "I think I made that pretty clear at the house too."

"Then why," I asked, "did you back up Willa in the movie theater parking lot?"

Owen's expression changed for a second—his protective armor failed, and I saw something like panic flash in his eyes. But he quickly sat up straighter, taking in a deep breath through his nose. "I'm entitled to change my mind," he said.

"You seemed pretty sure when I saw you at the house," I pointed out, "that there was no case to solve. It seemed like you'd felt that way for a while."

Owen scowled. "Do you have a little sister?" he asked.

"No," I said, not sure what that had to do with anything.

"She *never* gives up," Owen went on. "Willa *never* stops badgering me. So I knew if I didn't let her try to sell you on Izzy having this 'problem,' she'd drive me nuts. With you working on it, I figured she'd calm down."

I frowned at him. "At the movie theater, you said Izzy was acting strange. *Darker*, somehow."

"She is," he said. "She's just faking it."

I shook my head. "But yesterday you sent around a video of Gavin Yoo."

Owen furrowed his brows. "I did," he said.

I went on, "So you think they're *both* faking it? Gavin *and* Izzy?"

Owen turned his face away and shrugged. "I guess so," he said. "I got that video of Gavin from some guys at school. A lot of people were talking about it. It was a *thing.*"

I nodded. "And how did Gavin know I was looking for him yesterday?" I asked. Owen swallowed; I watched the lump travel down his throat. "Because it's clear that he knew," I said. "But I only told Willa I was planning to talk to him. And the direct link between Willa and Gavin would be . . . you."

Owen gazed out the windshield for a few seconds more and coughed. Finally he turned back to me, not quite meeting my eyes. "What exactly are you accusing me of here?"

I lowered my voice, forcing him to lean in. "When I saw you at the haunted house," I said calmly, "you said you had told your friends about Izzy and taken them there."

"So *what?*" Owen demanded, his voice getting sharp. "They were just looking to have some fun."

I didn't reply for a few seconds, giving him a hard stare. He twitched uncomfortably, staring back. Finally I said, "It just seems like a lot of the rumors about kids getting messed up at the house on Heliotrope Lane are coming from you."

Something lit in Owen's eyes—I was on to something. But he looked surprised that I'd figured this out—and not in a happy way.

"Do you have something to gain from kids wanting to go there?" I asked. "I mean, are you charging admission, or—"

Owen suddenly contracted in his seat like a spring snapping back into place. *"Go away,"* he said, his voice deepening into a growl. "I'm done humoring you. I don't have to answer your questions."

I just sat there, not moving an inch. "Maybe you'd like to talk to the police instead," I said in the same calm voice.

But Owen surprised me then; he pushed back in his seat and started to laugh. If he'd looked threatened before, that fear was gone now. He shook his head.

It unnerved me. "What are you laughing at?" I asked.

Owen laughed for another few seconds before answering, "Talk to the police about *what*?"

I frowned. "This whole thing," I replied, like it was obvious. "Izzy, and the house, and whatever—"

Owen cut me off with another sharp chuckle. "What charge would the police be holding me on, Nancy Drew?" he asked, looking me in the eye. His expression was different now. His eyes looked darker, harder. "Telling scary stories about a haunted house?" he asked, then suddenly moved a little closer to me.

I jumped back.

"Gossiping?" he pressed.

I scratched the foot that remained outside the car against the pavement; was he crazy? *No, he's not,* I realized. *He's right.* I had the terrible sense that Owen was involved in all this, somehow—but how could I prove it?

Telling scary stories wasn't a crime. Trespassing on abandoned property was a crime—but it was one I was guilty of too. And it wasn't like the police weren't aware that dozens of kids were in and out of the Furstenberg house each week.

The truth was, beyond the trespassing and possibly telling some lies, I wasn't sure a crime was being committed here at all.

Owen started laughing again, then reached out to start the car and pull his seat belt over his chest. "I'm gonna go now, Nancy Drew," he said. "Since you were so worried about me driving you to some secret location, you might want to get out now." He flashed me an insincere smile. His eyes were still dark and hard. "Have a nice day."

He threw the car into reverse, and, grabbing my purse, I struggled up and jumped clear of the car just in time to avoid having my foot run over as he backed up. The passenger-side door was still flapping open, and he paused, leaned over, and closed it before driving on out of the parking lot.

I could feel myself fuming as I watched the car disappear over a hill.

I'll get you, I promised myself, gritting my teeth.

I will get you, Owen—and if Gavin won't talk to me, maybe someone else will.

"Oh, *hello*, Izzy."

A few hours later I was sitting in Izzy's living room with her mom when Izzy walked in the door, arriving home from dance class.

Izzy stared at me as though I were an actual demon. *She knows who I am,* I realized. *And not just as the market researcher who cornered her about scary movies.*

I shot a look at her mother. "I was just telling your mom," I said, smiling toothily, "how I'm on the high school student council and how you're helping me set up for the high school orientation for middle schoolers at the end of the year. Anyway, I just wanted to go over a couple of ideas with you, Iz."

Izzy looked furious, as I'd expected, but she pasted on a smile for her mom. "Sure," she said, looking at me brightly. "Why don't we go talk in my room?"

I got up and said good-bye to her mom, then followed Izzy down a narrow hallway to a big, green-painted bedroom at the back of their house.

As soon as I was completely inside, Izzy reached behind me and shut the door. "What are you *doing* here?" she hissed. "You *told* Willa you wouldn't come. Willa is going to be furious!"

I looked at Izzy, trying to make my face the picture of cool, calm, and collected. "Is she?" I asked. "And just how would *you* know what I told Willa? Did Willa tell you herself, or did she tell Owen, and Owen passed it along?"

Izzy turned red. "I—she—what are you—"

I'd hit a nerve. As she sputtered, I looked around the room. A full-size bed was covered with a chevron-striped comforter, a shelf bearing several horror-themed DVDs hung on the opposite wall over an old tube television, and a somewhat newer DVD player and movie posters—*The Blair Witch Project*, a movie called *Final Warning*—decorated the walls.

"*Final Warning*. I just saw that movie with my friends. It was a Freaky Friday double feature," I said, pointing to the poster. Izzy looked even more confused.

"Actually," I went on, "there's a girl in that movie who gets possessed by an evil spirit—and she *kind of* acts a lot like you've been acting! When you're acting possessed, that is."

I turned back from the poster and frowned at her.

"That's—that's a coincidence," Izzy said, smoothing her hair behind her ear. Her eyes still looked wild.

I nodded. "Hmmm. Well, the thing is, also—if you were truly possessed by some kind of evil spirit or whatever role you're trying to sell, Izzy, you probably would have attacked me in your living room rather than pasting on a smile for your parents and then sniping at me in your bedroom." I paused, and Izzy's expression turned ferocious—a combination of frustration and anger.

"In fact," I said, "if you were *really* possessed, you probably would act just as violent with your parents as you do with other kids, right? But then, people who are really possessed—if that's possible—probably don't care about getting in trouble for trespassing."

I folded my arms in front of me and smiled. Izzy

glared at me, then seemed to reach some sort of decision and tipped her chin up. When she spoke, her voice was the same creepy, raspy, gargled-with-rocks voice that both she and Gavin had used before.

"WE don't like girls who question us," she began. . . .

But I just shook my head and laughed. "It's too late, Izzy," I said, gently pushing her aside and reaching for the doorknob. "I got what I came for."

Before I opened the door, I turned back to Izzy. I could see the wheels turning in her mind—she was trying to figure out what this meant, how much trouble she was in.

"I don't know why you're faking it," I said quietly, "but now I'm *sure* that you are."

CHAPTER NINE

An Invitation

THAT NIGHT I FELL ASLEEP PRACTICALLY on top of my laptop. I'd downloaded *Final Warning* and watched it again, and now I was sure—both Izzy and Gavin had stolen their "possessed by a demon" acts from that movie. But *why?* I'd fallen down an Internet rabbit hole, Googling things like *fake demon possession why* and *why make a haunted house*. While these searches had led me to some interesting Halloween party ideas, I wasn't really any closer to answering my question.

Finally, sleep seemed to decide it wasn't going to

just wait around for me and knocked me out flat. I wasn't even aware of dreaming—until I heard it.

Loud, evil-sounding laughter. Almost like a *cackle*.

I sat straight up in bed, startled awake. At first I figured I'd been having a nightmare, but then the sound came again.

Hoo hoo ha ha ha HA HA . . .

It seemed to be coming from outside the house.

Right outside the front door, actually.

I tiptoed out of bed, pulled on a robe, and quietly started down the stairs. Suddenly a dark figure moved in the hallway, and I stifled a scream, but still let out a huge gasp.

"Nancy?" a familiar voice called. The figure turned on a flashlight and shined it in my direction.

"Hannah?" I replied.

She was standing at the foot of the stairs in her striped flannel pj's. "Did you hear it too?" she asked.

"The laugh?" I asked. "It was super creepy . . . and really loud. It woke me up."

"Me too," Hannah said. "It sounded like it was

coming from just out here." She shined the beam of her flashlight in the direction of the front door.

I walked down the rest of the stairs and joined her at the front door. "Should we open it?" I whispered.

Hannah nodded. "I brought something else," she said, putting the flashlight down on the hallway table and picking up her heavy wooden rolling pin. "If anyone is out there . . ." She swung the rolling pin down in a motion that *definitely* looked like it could knock a bad guy out.

"Good call," I whispered, thinking, *Dang, maybe I should be bringing Hannah out sleuthing with me instead of Bess and George.*

"I'll open it, then," I whispered. "You be ready."

I unbolted the door, then put my hand on the doorknob and slowly, carefully turned it and pulled.

I was shaking in spite of myself as I looked outside—scared of seeing something huge, leering, and evil right on the front steps. I didn't *think* it would be a ghost or anything—but I wasn't completely ruling it out.

"Oh," Hannah said, and I murmured, "Yeah."

Because there was nothing and nobody. I grabbed the flashlight from the table and shined it across the front lawn, into the bushes near the house, around the cars parallel parked on the street. But nothing moved— not even a squirrel.

I could feel my breathing start to slow down.

"Nancy," Hannah said, "look."

She was pointing the end of her rolling pin at the top step. The flashlight illuminated a simple white envelope with the word *NANCY* written in uneven red block letters. My heart gave a little squeeze of fear, but I reached down, picked it up, and retreated back into the house, gesturing for Hannah to follow. Then I closed and locked the front door, turned off the flashlight, and put it back down on the table.

After hesitating for just a moment, I slid a finger under the envelope's seal.

"What is it?" Hannah asked. "Who would leave you a note in the middle of the night?"

I pulled out the note, written in the same creepy red letters as my name, and read it out loud:

"'If you want the truth, meet us at the house now. Come alone.'"

"What on earth?" Hannah asked. "Who wrote this to you?"

I shook my head. "Don't worry, Hannah," I said. "It's just a case I'm working on. Not a big deal."

"It's a big deal when they come to the house and make scary noises in the middle of the night," Hannah said, gesturing to the front door. She moved closer, and her eyes widened with concern. "You won't go anywhere alone, will you? Nancy. That would be a very bad idea. Please, promise me."

I looked up at her. "Okay," I whispered, "I promise. Don't worry, Hannah." I crammed the note back into the envelope and shoved it into the pocket of my robe. "I'll deal with this later. We can both go back to bed."

Hannah looked a bit skeptical at first, but then she nodded and smiled. "I know you are a smart girl, Nancy," she said. "All right. Sleep well, then."

She headed down the hallway toward her bedroom off the kitchen, still carrying her rolling pin.

As soon as she was out of sight, I darted back upstairs to my room and began throwing on the clothes I'd been wearing that day.

I hadn't lied to Hannah—I wouldn't. I wasn't going anywhere *alone*, per se . . . but I was definitely going to have to sneak out of the house.

After waiting long enough for Hannah to fall back asleep, then sneaking as silently as possible out the side door and hopping into my car, I watched George pull into a small parking lot at a church we'd found about a block from the house on Heliotrope Lane. Bess waved at me from the passenger seat, her mouth tight. I knew she couldn't be thrilled to be back here—the last place on earth she wanted to go.

The truth was, I wasn't really either.

I walked over to their car. George unlocked the doors and I slid into the back seat.

"So *what* happened exactly?" George asked.

"Yeah, you confronted Izzy?" Bess demanded,

giving me a quizzical look. "You confronted *Owen*?"

I tried to explain the events of the afternoon as briefly as possible: how I suspected that Owen was profiting in some way from talking up the haunted house and spreading rumors, and how I was almost 100 percent sure that Izzy was faking her "possession."

"And then you got a note?" George asked, the streetlights from the parking lot casting her face in sharp shadows. "They just left it at your front door in the middle of the night?"

I pulled the envelope from my jacket pocket and handed it to George. "They made a big point of waking me up with creepy cackling," I said. "They also woke up Hannah, unfortunately. I had to be a little misleading with her, to get out of the house."

Bess raised her eyebrows at me. "A little misleading?" she asked. "Is that Nancy-speak for *lying*?"

"No, not lying. I just told her I wouldn't come here alone."

George, who'd been studying the note, shoved it at

Bess. "Well, I'm glad we're here, under the circumstances," she said. "Who knows what Izzy and Owen are up to?"

I nodded as Bess took the note and read it over, biting her lip. "They must know I'm on to them, or at least part of what they're doing," I said. "Now I hope I can get to the bottom of this, once and for all."

Bess finished studying the note and handed it back to me with a little disbelieving shake of her head. "What would you like us to do, Nancy?" she asked. "If we go in there with you, they'll know right away you didn't follow their instructions."

"But you can't actually go in *alone*," George insisted. "That's way too dangerous."

"That's why I have a plan," I said, taking out my phone. I dialed George's number, held it up to show them, and then pressed call. George shook her head, then scrambled for her phone, which was in her car's cup holder, and picked it up.

"Hello, Nancy?" she answered. "I'm right here. You could just *tell* us your master plan."

"This *is* my master plan," I said into the phone.

Then I clicked the sleep button to darken the screen and stuck my phone back in my pocket, zipping it shut. "This way, you guys can listen in on my visit from your car. If you hear anything strange, you can run in after me—or call the police."

George put her phone back into the cup holder, nodding slowly. "Not bad," she said.

But Bess's furrowed brow told me she was still skeptical. "I dunno," she said. "It's not a *perfect* plan. If you got clonked over the head with a pipe or something, it would be too late for us to help you."

I rolled my eyes. "I'll be on the lookout for swinging pipes, just for you, Bess."

Bess sighed. "Don't get me wrong, Nancy. The phone plan is probably better than nothing." She paused, then added earnestly, "But if you're gone more than twenty minutes, we're coming in after you. Got it? No exceptions."

"Thanks, Bess," I said. "It means a lot to me that you'd charge in there after me, knowing how much you hate the place."

Bess nodded, but I saw her shiver a little. "I wish I could say that feeling has changed, Nancy, but it still feels—"

"I know," I said, cutting her off before she could say the word "evil." I wanted to believe there was nothing evil about the house. That it was all part of some elaborate plan.

But my gut had other beliefs.

"Anyway," I said, "I think I'd better get in there. But thank you, guys. You always have my back."

"Anytime, Nancy." George pointed to her phone. "You're not alone. We're just a few seconds' run away."

I tried not to think about how far the church was from the house, really, and how much could happen in a couple of seconds. *It's fine. It's just some teenagers playing games.*

"I'll remember," I said, opening the car door and climbing out. "Thanks again."

I walked back over to my car and drove the last block to the Furstenberg house. Surprisingly, there were no other cars parked nearby. *Assuming Owen is involved . . . how did he get here?*

As I got out of the car, I noticed that the block was entirely silent—not a bird chirping, no breeze stirring the trees. It felt like the neighborhood itself was holding its breath, waiting for something to happen.

I looked at the house. I felt the same sick feeling in my gut that I'd had the first time I saw it. It looked so sad, so abused . . . *if I were an angry ghost, this is where I'd live.* I felt a coldness wash over me, and gave an involuntary shiver.

I'd all but proven that Izzy was faking her strange behavior—which meant Gavin probably was too. But that didn't explain the eerie feeling I'd had of being watched when I picked up my car here before, or how unsettled I felt inside. I remembered standing with George in the basement, trying to open the locked room where Mrs. Furstenberg's body was supposedly found. Who'd locked the room, when none of the rest of the house was protected from trespassers? And why?

Did something terrible happen to Mrs. Furstenberg in this house? And is she trying to tell someone about it?

Forcing my feet into motion, I stepped onto the lawn and began walking around the house, toward the back and the open window.

I intend to find out, I told myself.

CHAPTER TEN

Answers

IT'S JUST A HOUSE. IT'S JUST A HOUSE.

I tried to remember my dad's words as I climbed through the broken window alone, for the first time, and came to stand in Mrs. Furstenberg's living room.

I took in a breath. The living room looked much the same as it had when Bess, George, and I had come here before, though there were a few new empty soda cans scattered on the tables, and a huge, half-empty bag of potato chips. I saw something quarter-size skitter out of the bag and run under what was left of the stained, blue-flowered couch, and I felt a shudder run through my body.

Oh, please let this be quick.

I looked around, wondering where Owen or Izzy or whoever planned on confronting me would be. There was no sign that someone was currently *here* in the house—all the furniture, or what remained of the furniture, was as we'd left it. I glanced at my reflection in the shattered mirror and shuddered. I remembered the lack of cars in front and wondered, all at once, whether this was all part of the elaborate practical joke: convince everyone the house is haunted, and then drag poor Nancy Drew there in the middle of the night to freak herself out. Was somebody filming me right now? Was I going to end up on *America's Funniest Home Videos*?

With a groan, I realized that I'd been so intent on getting here quickly, and coming up with the phone plan, that I'd forgotten to grab a flashlight. With shaking hands, I unzipped the pocket of my jacket and pulled out my phone, waking it up and then pressing the touch screen to turn on the flashlight feature. A narrow beam shot out of the back. It wasn't as bright as a *real* flashlight, but it would do.

So where are they? I shined the light down the hallway toward the bedrooms, and then gingerly stepped closer. The smell of mold filled my nostrils, and I looked around at the peeling striped wallpaper. I walked down to the first bedroom—Henry's, I remembered—and stepped inside.

It was the same as the last time we'd been there: wooden bed with broken slats, dresser, *Blood Fight* poster. Now I noticed that the *Blood Fight* poster had been vandalized with some kind of tag in silver Sharpie. I suddenly remembered the rodent trespasser we'd found in this room when I'd come with Bess and George, and I quickly backed into the hall.

Nothing to see here. Wouldn't want to wake anyone up. . . .

Wait, rats were nocturnal, right?

I shivered and hustled down the hallway.

I thought I heard something move in the living room and froze. I took in a slow breath through my nose, trying to calm myself, and glanced back, but there was no other noise. I was figuring I'd imagined it when I looked into Mrs. Furstenberg's bedroom and stifled a scream.

COME TO THE BASEMENT was spray-painted on the wall in bloodred paint that dripped down onto the wallpaper.

AAAAAUUGGH!

I felt my heart leap into my throat and dropped my phone, which of course made a huge clattering noise. When I leaned down and picked it up, still breathing hard, I could hear George asking, "Nancy? Are you okay?" even though I didn't have the speaker on.

"I . . . everything's going fine," I stammered, realizing at the last second that I should make it sound like I was talking to myself, just in case anyone was watching and listening. "Nothing to be afraid of. It seems like they want me to 'come to the basement,' so that's what I'll do, no need to fear."

Slowly, I stepped out of the bedroom, then down the ruined hallway back to the living room. I half expected someone to be hiding behind the edge of the couch, watching me, but there was no one and no sign that anyone had passed through there in the last few minutes. I walked through the living room to the kitchen. A tree right outside the window swayed in the breeze, casting flashing, deep shadows across the room.

The narrow door next to the stove was closed. I walked over to it and put my hand on the knob.

Don't do this, said a voice deep inside me.

Doing my best to ignore that voice, I pulled the door open.

Inside, the basement looked impossibly dark. I aimed my phone-flashlight down, but the beam was only strong enough to illuminate a couple of steps in front of me. As I descended, I looked around the big main room, but no one was there.

Or no one wants me to know they're there.

I had a sudden horrible feeling. *What if they're just waiting in the dark—waiting to grab me when I walk by?*

Panicked, I reached the foot of the stairs and began frantically beaming my faux-flashlight all over the place, trying to discern anything that looked out of the ordinary. But there was nothing. Now that my eyes were beginning to adjust, the moonlight shining through the tiny window illuminated the room just enough to see—

—there was no one there.

COME TO THE BASEMENT. That's what the wall said, right?

Why?

Then I glanced over and saw it. The tiniest sliver of flickering light—shining through a cracked door.

The door to the room where Mrs. Furstenberg's body had been found.

The room that had been closed off the last time we were here.

The light flickered again, and I felt my heart contract. My legs felt like lead. As much as I understood that I needed to go in there—that going inside was the only way to get the answers I so desperately wanted—not a single part of my body felt like that was a good idea. I wanted to run, screaming, up the stairs. I wanted to dive through that window, bolt across the lawn to my car, and jump in and *drive*.

And never come back.

But, said a tiny voice inside me. *But Willa.*

I knew I needed to get answers, if not for myself, then for her. Even if Izzy was faking it, I believed that the fear Willa felt for her friend was real. She deserved answers, just like I did. Just like the police did. Just like Mrs. Furstenberg did.

I lifted my phone closer to my lips. "Okay," I said, and my voice came out all high and shaky. "It seems like someone's in this little room, the one that used to be closed. Crazy! But I'm sure there's nothing to be afraid of. Here I go . . ."

I forced myself to move, and then I heard it again. *Cackling.* The same evil laughter I'd heard outside my front door earlier. But this time, it wasn't a sharp sound—instead, it seemed to travel all over the room. *Hoo hoo ha HA HA HA . . .* I couldn't tell where it was coming from—from behind me on the stairs, from outside, from inside the tiny, formerly locked room?

Or from inside your own head, Nancy?

Maybe all of the above.

It felt like someone was not only watching me—they were laughing at me.

Somehow, moving more slowly than I would have thought possible, I reached the edge of the door. The flickering light seemed brighter here—candles, maybe? I could smell something dry and sulfuric inside. I reached out my hand, trembling like crazy, and pushed open the door.

"Okay," I said shakily, stepping over the threshold. "Here I come . . ."

I could just make out dark walls illuminated by a flickering light.

Before I could see anything else, I was suddenly grabbed from behind, and a huge, black-gloved hand was clamped over my mouth!

CHAPTER ELEVEN

Guess Who?

I WAS TOO STARTLED TO EVEN TRY TO scream.

Whoever grabbed me turned me around to face them and I stood staring, the gloved hand now firmly holding onto my arm.

I was facing someone—a teenager or adult, from the size of him or her—wearing a black sheet and a terrifying monster mask. The mask depicted a demon-type creature with red eyes, gray skin, and curving horns. Then the figure let out a low laugh— deep, raspy, the same gargling-with-rocks effect that

Izzy and Gavin had used when they were acting "possessed."

It was male, I was pretty sure.

He suddenly started patting me down with his free hand, like I'd been pulled out of the TSA line at the airport for a "special screening."

"What are you doing?" I shouted and instinctively pulled away, but it was too late.

He'd felt my car keys and phone through my jacket and shoved his hand into my pocket, pulling them out. He held them up, dangling them in front of me, and slowly shook his head. When he saw the phone had a call going, he very purposefully poked a finger on the end call button, hanging up on Bess and George.

I watched him type a message to George from my phone: EVERYTHING'S OKAY! JUST SOME PRANK. LOW BATTERY. LET'S MEET AT MY HOUSE IN THE MORNING. Then he turned my phone off.

My heart fell into my stomach. Would my friends believe that?

"What are you doing?" I demanded, summoning

up all my anger and courage to glare at him. "You can't do that!"

But the figure didn't say anything. He just released my arm and stood back, watching me through the eyes of that creepy mask. It was too dark to make out his eye color. But I could hear his breathing, even and loud in the near-silent basement.

He wasn't feeling nervous. He was in control.

And I was getting the message loud and clear. If I wanted my things back, I wasn't getting into that room. And I would never learn the truth about what was going on in this house.

I hesitated. A *huge* part of me wanted to take my things and go. Whatever creepy game this guy was playing, I didn't need to be part of it. I could be home, fast asleep and not worrying about ghosts or haunted houses or cranky teenagers at *all*.

But then I sighed, realizing that I couldn't do that. Because I thought of Mrs. Furstenberg, who had lived a huge part of her life in this house, even died here. This was her home, and now it was being destroyed by vandals. Nobody even knew the truth about how she died.

I owed it to her to find out what I could.

I owed it to Willa to find out why her friend was scaring her.

It was time *somebody* got to the bottom of this. And it looked like the only willing "somebody" was me.

So I put my hands down and nodded at the demon—*okay.*

He nodded back, seeming satisfied, and pushed me toward the door to the smaller room.

I walked inside very slowly. The room was very small and was lit by a single candle sitting on a stool in the middle of the room. The walls were dark cement, like the rest of the basement, lined with empty metal shelves.

At first I didn't see anyone. A shard of panic pierced my heart, and I swiveled back toward the door, wondering if the demon was going to lock me in—

But then I heard soft laughter, and turned back around to see another black-sheeted figure—this one wearing a zombie mask with yellow eyes and a deep cut down the side of its face—step forward from the side of the room. As my eyes adjusted, I saw two more black-sheeted figures, these ones wearing a witch mask and a werewolf mask, still standing in the shadows. And the figure who had grabbed me outside followed me in without shutting the door.

"So you think you know the truth." The one in the zombie mask suddenly spoke, using the same "possessed" voice that was so familiar to me now—the same one, I now realized, that had been used in the cult horror movie *Final Warning*.

I lifted my chin, straightened my back, and faced the figure who was speaking, hoping I looked unafraid.

"You think this is a hoax," the figure went on. *"But can you be* sure?*"*

Pretty sure, I thought but didn't say.

He or she stepped closer. *"If someone dies in a horrible way, with an abundance of pain, anger, or fear, isn't it possible that their fear and anger would still exist—that they could infect others?"*

I just stared at him or her, not responding. *What are you getting at?* I wondered.

The figure stepped even closer. I felt a flutter of fear but didn't move.

"What if I were to kill you right here?"

I swallowed hard, suddenly scared witless, but I willed myself not to move.

The figure cackled quietly, amused by my fear. *"Wouldn't you like to believe, Nancy Drew, that you would be able to get revenge somehow?"* Pause. Step closer. He or she was only a couple of feet away now. *"Even if it had to be from the afterlife?"*

Now I felt an answer bubbling up inside of me. It seemed obvious. "No," I said, a little more forcefully than I'd intended.

The figure tilted its masked head, regarding me curiously.

"If I were killed, I would want to find peace, somehow." I glanced from the main figure to the two still standing off to the side—and the one who had grabbed me outside the room and now stood in the doorway, watching.

I took in another breath, then said, "Owen and Izzy are taking advantage of people's fears. They're trying to convince others that this place is haunted—I *know* that. What I don't know is why."

The zombie mask stood very still for a moment, watching me. *"Why do you think?"* he or she asked finally, in the same raspy voice.

"I guess . . . ," I began, a plan forming in my mind. I tensed my muscles, getting ready. "I guess . . . they must have something to gain."

The zombie mask cackled again, louder this time, and I lunged forward, reaching out my hands toward him or her. The other figures rushed toward me, reaching out to grab me, but they were too late—I'd grabbed the edge of the lead figure's mask. As he or she struggled to throw me off, and one of the others grabbed my elbow, I pulled with all my might, and just managed to yank the mask off. The rubber shell came off in my hands, and suddenly I was looking into a real person's face.

It wasn't Owen or Izzy.

It was a man.

When I managed to get the mask off, it was like all the air had gone out of the room. The figure who'd grabbed my elbow dropped my arm, and the three of them backed away, as though watching to see what I would do.

The man looked startled for a moment—but then his face transformed into an expression of pure, crazed amusement. To my surprise, he dropped the raspy cackle and started laughing—a real, overpowering, and seriously unhinged laugh.

Then he stopped, stared right at me, and demanded, "Do you recognize me?"

A chill crept up my spine as I realized I did.

His face had been all over the news reports I'd seen online.

"You're Henry Furstenberg," I whispered, right as two of the other figures grabbed me and dragged me away.

CHAPTER TWELVE

Showdown

"YOU'RE A SHARP ONE."

Henry Furstenberg smiled at me, but his compliment didn't bring any pleasure. I was still being held by the other two masked figures, and my heart was dancing a rhumba inside my chest as terrified thoughts tumbled through my head. *What is Henry Furstenberg doing here?*

Did he kill his mother?

Am I standing in front of a murderer?

"You're right, Nancy: I am Henry Furstenberg. As I'm sure you've heard from the police and others, they've been searching for me for over a year—ever since my mother's unfortunate passing." He licked his lips. His demeanor was precise, careful . . . *A perfectionist for sure*, I thought. "I've been in hiding."

"Why?" I asked. Henry's gaze shot back to me, annoyed, but I kept going. "Did you kill her? Is that why you were hiding?"

He stared at me for a moment, and I couldn't tell whether his dark eyes held surprise or anger. Finally he shook his head. "Did I kill her? Oh, Nancy Drew, how pleasant it must be to live in such a black-and-white world." He paused, looking at the candle. "I lived here with my mother for a long time. It was very difficult for me, not that anyone seems to care about that. Have you ever lived with an aging person?"

I wasn't sure how to respond to that. *We're all aging, all the time?* But I guessed he meant an elderly person, a person whose health was declining, like his mother's. "No," I said.

He stepped forward, his nostrils flaring. "It is *very difficult*," he repeated. "When I first moved in, she was self-sufficient. But as she aged, she began needing help getting out of a chair, then out of bed, then even getting dressed or taking a shower. She had trouble navigating the stairs, and she lost her vision, making it impossible for her to drive. I went from being an independent adult to being a full-time caregiver. It was a huge sacrifice for me—and *not* something I volunteered for."

I stared at him. I was getting the sense that at the very least, Henry was a very selfish person. At worst, he had a few screws loose.

"I guess it's payback," I couldn't help saying, though I realized it probably wouldn't help my cause. "They take care of you for eighteen years, you know, feeding you, nursing you, teaching you how to walk. The least we can do is . . . repay the favor?"

Anger flared in Henry's eyes, but his outward expression didn't change. "I suppose that's one perspective," he said. Then he held his fist to his mouth, letting out a short cough. "*Anyway.* One day I followed my mother into the basement, where she was *insisting* on doing my laundry as well as hers."

Oh, was she? I thought. Henry didn't seem the type of guy to volunteer.

"I told her," he said, "I said, *please* do not put my delicate garments in the dryer. It was an ongoing argument we had. When she was younger, she was very good about it. But as she declined . . ." He sighed. "Well, she was not as careful."

"So you killed her?" I challenged, not believing what I was hearing. "You killed her because you were afraid she would shrink your sweater or something?"

He glared at me. His careful, precise outward demeanor disappeared, his eyes bulged, and his face turned bright red. "*I DIDN'T KILL HER!*" he suddenly screamed.

I couldn't help flinching at this unexpected outburst. Even the figures holding me seemed to do the same.

There was silence for a moment, as his face returned to normal, and then I said quietly, "I'm sorry."

He looked down at me, then seemed to straighten his shoulders and recover a bit.

"Tell me what really happened," I said.

He looked away, focusing his gaze on the metal shelving bolted to the opposite wall. "We argued," he said in a softer voice. "It became . . . heated. She ran in here. And then suddenly . . ."

He stopped for a moment and wiped his eye. He looked honestly pained. *Maybe I misjudged him?*

"She clutched her chest," he said with some difficulty, "and . . . she fell to the floor."

We were all silent as Henry looked down at some spot just above the floor. He seemed to be seeing something inside his mind.

"I am sorry to say that she died," he said finally, raising his chin to look me in the eye again.

"I'm so sorry," I said honestly.

He nodded shortly. His voice was stronger when he went on, "I knew that my mother had told her friends that she and I didn't get along. We argued . . . quite a bit. I was terrified, you see—I thought I would be blamed for her death." He swallowed. "I panicked and ran. I did not realize at the time that my mother left no will, and with me missing, the house fell into disrepair while an heir was located."

He sighed. "My own foolishness destroyed the value of what should have been my inheritance. And in the time I was gone, a cousin was found and the ownership of the house passed to her—although, as you can see, she did *nothing* to fix it up. The more I thought about it, the angrier I became. After the years I spent caring for my mother in the twilight of her life—I got nothing?"

He shot me a pleading look that I wasn't sure how to respond to. The house was destroyed because he'd disappeared, taking off with his mother's body still cooling in the basement. *Poor you?*

"So I came up with a plan," Henry said, seeming to gain some swagger back. He put his hands on his hips. "I realized I could drive down the value of the house even further if I could convince people it was haunted. Teenagers were the perfect targets—they spread rumors like wildfire. And just as I planned, kids have been pouring in and causing all kinds of damage along the way—if the house didn't look haunted before, it certainly does now!"

I stared at him, stunned. *You destroyed your own house?*

"So I could buy this house for the proverbial song. I could flip it or tear it down. Endless possibilities," he went on, "I reached out to Owen, who'd done yard work for us when Mother was alive, via Facebook. I knew that Owen was the perfect person to contact, because we'd occasionally discussed that he's a horror movie enthusiast and even wants to be a director someday. He pulled in fellow horror movie fans Gavin and Izzy, and I've promised to pay them handsomely for their efforts—seed money to shoot a movie of their own." He paused. "But . . . there was a problem."

"Willa," I murmured, realizing where this was going.

He nodded. One of the figures holding me—Owen?—shook his head and sighed.

"We thought that Willa would be just the right person to spread the word," Henry went on. "She and

Izzy are very close, and Willa is a very . . . trusting soul. But soon after the act began, it became clear that Willa might be a problem. She felt personally threatened and grew frightened for her friend. We think that Izzy's 'possessed' act may have been a little *too* convincing. Willa was clearly worried, and she wanted to hire you, Nancy. Owen and I decided to allow it, because it would quiet her concerns, and besides, how effective could a teenage sleuth be?" He chuckled. "Owen has kept me up-to-date on your progress as you worked on the case. But when it became clear that we couldn't scare you away, and you were getting close to the truth, I realized that my plan required some adjusting. . . ."

I felt a chill. *Where is this going?*

Henry stopped, then gave me an almost disarming smile. "So, I believe congratulations are in order! You see, I was able to speed along the sale. I had to pay a bit more for it than originally intended but the insurance policy I attained should more than make up for that." He paused to pat my head, "I'm so sorry, Nancy." His eyes didn't look sorry. "It's your own fault, you know. If only you had left things alone."

I stumbled, feeling sick. *What are they going to . . .*

Henry looked behind me, to the still-open door. "Fortunately," he said, "my mother's house comes equipped with an excellent detention area. We'll simply leave you in this room and lock it when we leave." He cackled again—not quite the raspy "possessed" cackle of before, but definitely along those lines. The sound chilled my blood. "No one can hear you scream down here. Even if they could, they would simply assume it's the 'ghost' that everyone knows haunts this house! And when your burned remains are found—the police will just assume you were trespassing in the haunted house and accidentally caused the fire. Then I will get a great big check."

He smiled, and his smile was full-on evil now— eyes full of fury.

He began walking toward me.

"How did you come up with your plan?" I blurted, thinking, *Keep him talking, Nancy—you know that works!* "It's, um, very clever, the whole idea of driving down—"

"Oh, *shut up.*" Henry scowled, and it was clear from his expression that whatever amusement I'd offered up till this point had expired. "Do you think I don't know what you're doing? Trying to keep me talking all night long about my 'master plan'? Well, forget it. You're sharp, but I'm even sharper—and I'm going to dispose of you now."

"Owen . . . Gavin . . . Izzy . . . whoever you are," I pleaded. "You know this isn't right! Don't let him to do this to me!"

None of them moved, and the two who were holding me continued to do so. The one on the left, the one who'd originally grabbed me and taken my phone, stared at Henry. He seemed to be thinking.

Finally he pulled off his mask—*Owen!*

"Henry," he said quietly, "no one was supposed to get hurt. Maybe we should—"

"*Shut up!*" Henry hissed, turning to him with a look of utter disgust. "You're deep in this now, Owen.

Do you want me to reveal to the police all you've done? Trespassing, fraud . . . accessory to a murder?"

Owen looked alarmed for a second, and then his gaze turned blank. He slipped his mask back on, and his hold on my arm tightened.

I felt my heart thudding in my chest and found it hard to take a breath. They were going to leave me in this locked room to burn.

No!

In one determined motion, I managed to yank my arm out of Owen's grasp and swing it at the stool, sending the still-burning candle flying toward us. I ducked, and the flame caught on the other figure's sheet, sending larger flames roaring up his or her torso.

"No!" Gavin's voice cried. His grip relaxed on my other arm.

"Wait," Izzy cried, pulling off the witch mask and running over. "We have to—"

I didn't wait to find out. Taking advantage of the chaos, I yanked away from Gavin and Owen and ran past them, darting out the door.

Henry followed me. I could hear and feel him behind me, panting, just a few steps away. But I managed to make it to the narrow stairway that led to the kitchen, and I reached out to grab a heavy snow shovel that hung from the wall. I thundered up the stairs, throwing open the door and internally rejoicing at the sight of moonlight coming through the windows.

Just as I was going to run through the kitchen and into the living room, something grabbed my left ankle and pulled. I let out a scream, turning and blindly swinging with the shovel. Henry let go of my ankle and grabbed the shovel's shaft, trying to push it back at me, but I struggled to free it from his grasp and raised the blade above my head. Even though he still held the shaft, I had enough space to send the blade crashing down on his head with all my might. He let out a yelp and fell back.

Shaking, I pulled the shovel back and looked at the blade. There was a dark spot I thought might be blood. I let out a trembling breath.

Then I heard scuffling from the living room.

"Nancy!" There was the thud of a pair of feet hitting the floor, followed by another pair.

"*Nancy!* Are you in here? We called the police!"

"We knew something was wrong. You *always* charge your phone!"

A rush of relief went through me. *Bess and George.* They knew. They'd called the police!

Just then the door to the basement stairs flew open and Henry stomped into the kitchen, blood trickling down his face from a wound on the side of his head. His eyes bulged. "You have friends here?" he asked in a creepy voice. "Excellent. I guess I'll just have to burn you all!"

"No!" I screamed, grabbing the shovel, but Henry was now holding a baseball bat he must have taken from someplace downstairs. Before I could swing at him, he lifted the bat over his head and I heard George scream, "Nancy, duck!"

I ducked. I could feel the breeze from the bat skimming by my face, and then the clatter of feet running into the kitchen.

"I'll get you for that!" Henry screamed. He hoisted the bat again as I aimed the shovel and—

SHHHHHHHHHHHH!

"AUUUUUUGH!" Henry suddenly screamed in agony. The bat fell to the floor as he sank down, landing in a sitting position.

"That's what you get!" an angry voice shouted. *Bess!* I looked up and found my scared-of-haunted-houses friend, brandishing a bottle of pepper spray like it was bug killer and the world's biggest cockroach was sitting right in front of her.

My mouth dropped open.

"Omigod, *Bess!*" George cried, as Henry covered his face with his hands and moaned some more. "You actually *carry* pepper spray? All this time, I thought you were just trying to threaten people with it to scare them!"

Bess turned to George, mindlessly pointing the pepper spray can at her. George flinched, and Bess shrugged and put the pepper spray back in her purse. "Of course I carry it, George," she said, gesturing with her elbow at Henry. "A girl can't be too careful these days."

George laughed, and I dropped my shovel to the floor, limp with relief. Because over the constant sound of Henry's moaning, and Bess and George's back-and-forth about the merits of Mace versus pepper spray, I heard a glorious sound.

Police sirens, several of them, distant at first, but then coming closer and closer. Within seconds, they were drawing close to the house on Heliotrope Lane.

CHAPTER THIRTEEN

Scary Movie 2

"WOW. IT LOOKS SO DIFFERENT," I MURMURED.

It was months after I'd confronted Henry Furstenberg in his own basement, and George, Bess, and I had returned to the site of the old house on Heliotrope Lane.

The house had been torn down, and work had just begun on the construction of a community center for the elderly. Mrs. Furstenberg's long-lost cousin, on learning what had happened to Mrs. Furstenberg, decided to donate the land to help elderly people.

"I think this new center is going to do a lot of

good," George said, nodding at the sign that proclaimed FUTURE HOME OF THE BEATRICE FURSTENBERG CENTER FOR SENIORS. "I was reading online that they're going to have art, cooking, and exercise classes, social groups . . . and social workers are going to come in once a week or so, in case seniors have any concerns they can address."

"That's really great," Bess said. "Maybe a center like this would have really helped Mrs. Furstenberg."

"Maybe," I agreed, watching the construction workers raise huge wooden piles to support the center's walls. I was still trying to accept that I would never know the truth about Mrs. Furstenberg's life, or death. I believed Henry when he said he hadn't killed her—and he'd remained consistent with that story, telling it over and over again when police, and family lawyers, questioned him about what happened to his mother. They'd argued, and she'd had a heart attack. But a part of me still felt terrible for poor old Mrs. Furstenberg. Henry clearly was a few tacos short of a combo platter. Living with him as her main caregiver for so many years couldn't have been easy.

In the end, Henry had been charged with attempted murder, trespassing, fraud, and a few other minor charges related to the haunted house hoax. The last I'd heard, his lawyer was arguing that he needed mental help, which I would certainly agree with. If a judge also agreed, he would be moved to a mental hospital for an indefinite term. If not, he faced a significant prison sentence.

Whatever happened, I trusted the courts to sort it out. *I just deliver them the crooks—they can decide what to do with them.*

"I saw Gavin the other day," Bess said. "He said his sessions with the therapist are really helping, and he's enjoying the community work he's been doing in a nursing home."

"That's great," I said. "I've heard through Willa that Owen's sessions are going well too. They have him teaching a film course to some kids at a family shelter, and it's helping him put things in perspective."

Despite Henry's threats the night he confronted me in the basement, neither Gavin nor Owen got in serious trouble for their role in the haunted house scam. Their lawyers settled for a deal where they would both testify against Henry, and they both got probation and had to see a counselor and do community service.

Bess glanced at me curiously. "How is Willa doing?" she asked. "You still think she really had no idea what her brother and best friend were up to, right?"

"That's right." Willa had been stunned by the news of what was really happening on Heliotrope Lane, and she had felt terribly betrayed by both her brother and her best friend. Like Gavin and Owen, Izzy was seeing a counselor, and after a rough patch, she and Willa made up and remained best friends. "She was totally sincere in everything she told me—including that Izzy would freak if I ever tried to talk to her parents. I think she's learned a lot from this experience—she won't be so trusting moving forward."

George frowned. "I *guess* that's a good thing."

"In a perfect world, everyone could be trusting all

the time," I said. "But this isn't a perfect world. Look what happened to Izzy, Owen, and Gavin—they trusted Henry."

Bess nodded. "Hey, what ever became of their movie?"

I smiled. Ah yes—the movie they planned to produce with the money Henry was going to pay them for acting possessed. "I think it's on indefinite hold," I said. "Willa says all three of them are still scary movie fans—but they're focusing on their studies for now. I think it freaked them all out a little to realize how far they had gone for their scary movie passion. It's time to get back to reality."

Bess and George agreed, and then suddenly the *ding* of George's phone in her pocket startled us. She reached in and pulled it out, holding the screen up to her face and smiling.

"Guys," she said, "amazing news! There's another horror movie festival coming up! This one goes on all weekend, and—"

Bess stopped her right there. "Are you kidding?

George, you remember what happened at the last scary movie, right?"

George looked at her quizzically. "It was really good?"

I laughed. *"And* we met Willa and Owen," I reminded her. *"And* it led to . . . some seriously scary moments."

George shook her head. "Come on guys, scary movies can be fun—at least in a movie, we all know that the haunting is, well, fake."

I sighed, then spoke up. "Okay—I'll go."

Bess raised her eyebrows. "Seriously, Nancy? You're ready to go back to another scary movie?"

"Really?" George asked, looking as stunned. "I have to be honest, you know—I was almost suggesting it as a joke." She paused. *"Almost."*

"Sure." I pointed to the small spray can dangling from Bess's key chain. "After all, what do I have to be afraid of? Bess just got a new can of pepper spray!"

Dear Diary,

I TOLD YOU I DON'T BELIEVE IN GHOSTS!
And now I remember why. Because there's always a logical explanation! Here, it was a greedy son, trying to drive down the cost of the house he thought he should have inherited. And I think Henry is a little unhinged, too. I hope that now he's in custody, he'll get the help he needs. And I'm glad that Willa and Izzy seem to be working things out. There's nothing more valuable in life than a good friend.

Speaking of which, thank goodness George and Bess—and Bess's pepper spray—were there to back me up. There's no one I'd rather face an angry "ghost" with than those two!